SHADOWS AT PREDATOR REEF

READ ALL THE MYSTERIES IN THE

HARDY BOYS ADVENTURES:

#1 *Secret of the Red Arrow*

#2 *Mystery of the Phantom Heist*

#3 *The Vanishing Game*

#4 *Into Thin Air*

#5 *Peril at Granite Peak*

#6 *The Battle of Bayport*

COMING SOON:

#8 *Deception on the Set*

HARDY BOYS ADVENTURES™

#7 SHADOWS AT PREDATOR REEF

FRANKLIN W. DIXON

ALADDIN New York London Toronto Sydney New Delhi

ALADDIN
An imprint of Simon & Schuster Children's Publishing Division
1230 Avenue of the Americas, New York, NY 10020
This Aladdin paperback edition October 2014

Also available in an Aladdin hardcover edition.
For information about special discounts for bulk purchases, please contact Simon & Schuster Special Sales at 1-866-506-1949 or business@simonandschuster.com.
The Simon & Schuster Speakers Bureau can bring authors to your live event.
For more information or to book an event contact the Simon & Schuster Speakers Bureau at 1-866-248-3049 or visit our website at www.simonspeakers.com.
Cover design by Karin Paprocki
The text of this book was set in Adobe Caslon Pro.
Manufactured in the United States of America 0914 OFF
2 4 6 8 10 9 7 5 3 1
Library of Congress Control Number 2013954635
ISBN 978-1-4814-0010-7 (hc)
ISBN 978-1-4814-0009-1 (pbk)
ISBN 978-1-4814-0011-4 (eBook)

CONTENTS

DIVE TIME

JOE

IT WAS THE LAST DIVE OF THE MORNING. FROM THE water's depths, I checked the air tank pressure on the high-tech dive computer I wore around my wrist like a watch and signaled to the other divers in preparation for my rise. It wasn't until I reached the surface that I saw the big gray dorsal fin slicing through the water and heading straight at me.

I could practically hear the *Jaws* theme music reverberating through my head as the fin grew larger and larger. I glanced around, but there was nowhere for me to go. The beast sped closer until its sleek gray snout rose out of the water mere inches from my face.

It was a huge . . . dolphin! The playful animal leaped over my head and slid back into the water on the other side, chattering happily.

“Great job on that last dive, Joe,” my supercute scuba instructor, Aly Hawke, called from the side of the ginormous water tank. “I think Scooter approves.”

“Well, I have an excellent teacher—” I started to reply just as Scooter the bottlenose dolphin spit a fountain of water in my face, ruining my attempt at being suave. I think he was jealous.

“Thanks, Aquaman,” Aly giggled. “Now hop on out, do an equipment check, and then you can head over to the reef for the opening-day celebration.”

Scooter gave my backside a helpful nudge as I climbed out of the dolphin tank at Bayport Aquarium, where I was taking a scuba certification course. I had a feeling diving skills would come in handy someday—and for more than just fun.

See, my brother Frank and I have this knack for solving mysteries. We’ve been doing it ever since we were kids in our hometown of Bayport, and over the years I’ve learned that it never hurts for a detective to know a few extra tricks. It might still be a while before Frank and I could get our investigators’ licenses (not that that ever stopped us before), but soon I’d be a card-carrying scuba diver.

Frank and I had both caught the ocean bug on our last big case, which had us spending a lot of time on the waterfront aboard a restored Revolutionary War ship. The ship was docked just across the harbor from the Bayport Aquarium, which had given Frank the idea of volunteering at the aquarium to help out with the grand opening of their new exhibit. Predator Reef was going to be the world's largest indoor habitat of its kind, designed by world-famous architect Bradley Valledor. Mobs of visitors and news media had been lining up all morning for the exhibit's big reveal.

Frank tried to get me to volunteer too, but I wasn't as interested in learning all that marine biology stuff he's always going on about (I get enough of that in science class, thanks!). But when he told me the aquarium was offering scuba-diving classes? Well, that's more my style. Exploration! Adventure! Danger! Not that diving in the dolphin tank was exactly dangerous. It was pretty mind-blowing, though. I think the technical term for it is "flipping awesome!" And it wasn't just the dolphins that were blowing my mind.

Aly was only a few years older than me, and she was already a master diver, so she was talented as well as pretty. And she really did look extra cute in her scuba gear. She had scheduled our class early so we could finish in time for Predator Reef's big ribbon-cutting ceremony at noon. She was taking part in the festivities too, diving in the tank to feed the fish along with the rest of the BAD team (that's what the Bayport Aquarium Divers call themselves).

I wasn't involved in the exhibit's prep and planning like Frank or Aly, but I was excited to see it. They were keeping it under wraps until the big unveiling, and from everything Frank had told me, it sounded totally out of this world:

hundreds of different species of sea animals, including a giant turtle, rays, and small sharks.

I was looking forward to seeing the BAD divers in action too, although not all of them were as enticing as Aly. There was one in particular I actually wouldn't have minded seeing eaten by a shark. Aly's ex-boyfriend Carter was as clueless as he was obnoxious. I really didn't know what she had seen in him—other than the fact that he was featured in national scuba-diving magazines and that all the girls at Bayport High seemed to be gaga over him.

Did I mention that I really, really don't like the guy?

When he showed up in the dolphin arena after class, it was almost enough to ruin my morning.

"Hey, babe," Carter called to Aly from the staff tunnel. "You done babysitting the newbies yet? We've got a hot date to get to."

Aly rolled her eyes. "Having to work together as dive buddies is not a date, Carter. And I'm not your babe anymore."

"Sure you are, you just don't realize it yet," he said. He looked so smug, I didn't need a special computer to know my annoyance meter was rising to dangerous levels.

"Show her some respect, man," I said as I packed up my dive kit.

"Mind your own business, newb." Carter didn't look so smug anymore. But he did look angry. I don't think Scooter was the only jealous one. "Babe, tell me you're not interested in this twerp?"

"You have water in your ears, Carter? I thought she asked you not to call her that." I stood my ground as he stalked toward me.

"Sheesh, knock it off, Carter," Aly said. "Joe is just taking my class. Besides, it's none of your business even if I was."

I have to admit that I liked the way that last part sounded. Now it was my turn to look smug. But Carter sure didn't like it. He might have actually been getting ready to do something about it too, but Scooter had the last word, slapping the pool with his tail and soaking us both in a sheet of water.

Aly laughed and gave Scooter a kiss on the nose. "Aw, my hero."

She looked back over her shoulder at Carter and me and shook her head as she walked off. "Boys."

I think just maybe the little sparkle in her eyes was meant for me.

Carter must have thought so too. He waited until Aly was out of earshot and stared me down before chasing after her.

"You'd better watch your back, newb," he said, just low enough so none of the other divers could hear. "You're gonna be fish food when I'm done with you."

INTO THE DEEP

2

FRANK

CORAL REEFS ARE THE CITIES OF THE sea," I told a group of kids and parents gathered around me. We were standing in front of a big blue curtain that was blocking the entire tank area; the curtain had PREDATOR REEF printed on it in bold letters surrounded by the silhouettes of circling sharks. When pulled back in a few minutes, the curtain would reveal the world's largest replica coral reef.

Joe sometimes makes fun of me because I get so psyched about this stuff, but how could you not? As an aquarium volunteer, I'd gotten a sneak peek at Predator Reef, and it was one of the coolest things I'd ever seen. With a whopping four hundred thousand gallons of salt water and thousands of beautiful and bizarre sea creatures, it was like entering another world.

"Reefs really are some of the world's most fascinating ecosystems," I continued, eager to share my enthusiasm with the kids. "Just like the houses and high-rises in a city, different types of coral provide homes for all kinds of fish—and each has a different job to do. Everything in the reef—from the tiniest clown fish to the biggest predators, like sharks—serves a purpose in an intricate web of life. Reefs aren't just beautiful and interesting, though; they're crucial to the health of the entire ocean, which is why it's so important to protect them."

And that was one of the big reasons I was so fired up about the new exhibit. The world's reefs and their inhabitants were disappearing at an alarming rate, and Predator Reef was going to be a great tool to teach people about the importance of conservation. All I had to do was look at the amazed expressions on the kids' faces, and I knew I was really getting the chance to inspire them.

Catching crooks would always be my first love, but after volunteering at the aquarium, I could also see myself becoming a marine biologist someday. "Frank Hardy, Deep-Sea Detective" has a nice ring to it.

During our last case, I'd been volunteering at the Bayport History Museum, a short water-taxi ride across the harbor from the aquarium. While I was still really interested in local history—in fact, later that week I was supposed to go on a tour of a tunnel that was used by the Underground Railroad to smuggle escaped slaves—it was nothing compared to the excitement I felt about Predator Reef.

The exhibit's humungous tank was going to be the centerpiece of the aquarium. It was designed so you could see it from above or below the surface depending on which level you were on. The surface of the tank filled the center of the aquarium's lobby so you could look straight down into the water from there or from any of the aquarium's upper levels. Even better, you could go down to the lower level to get an underwater view through a giant panoramic window that brought you face-to-face with all the different creatures. Skilled artists had sculpted synthetic coral for the exhibit, so no living reefs would be harmed collecting the real thing. The whole project really was like a bustling underwater city full of brightly colored fish of all sizes, along with trippy-looking rays; exotic bottom-dwelling zebra sharks with cute smiley faces and long, sail-like tails; and a whole school of ultra-sleek blacktip reef sharks.

The sharks weren't the main attraction, though. That honor went to the aquarium's unofficial mascot, a five-hundred-pound giant green sea turtle named Captain Hook. Captain Hook had gotten her name when a great white shark took a big bite out of one of her front flippers, leaving her with a skinny flipper that looked like a hook. Together with the black patch marking over her left eye, the name just seemed to fit.

The aquarium had made Captain Hook the main focus of Predator Reef's marketing campaign, featuring her in TV commercials, online videos, and billboards. Her sweet-natured personality was as big as she was. It was no wonder the kids in my tour group were itching to see her in person.

"When do we get to meet the big turtle?" one little girl asked.

I checked my watch and smiled. "It's almost time. Any minute now Predator Reef will come to life right before your eyes."

"Is that going to be the turtle's home?" another child asked.

"It sure is," I said, leaning down to the kids' level. "The aquarium rescued Captain Hook when she washed up on the beach and nursed her back to health. They normally would've had to release her back into the ocean, because green sea turtles are an endangered species, but the aquarium kept her because she would have had a hard time surviving in the wild with her injured flipper."

The kids were mesmerized. One little boy in a Captain Hook T-shirt jumped up and down, asking his mom if he could have a giant turtle too. It was really cool how Captain Hook had turned into a Bayport celebrity before the exhibit had even opened.

Her biggest fan was probably Bradley Valledor, the aquarium board member whose architecture firm had built the new exhibit. Mr. V, as everyone at the aquarium called him, fussed over Captain Hook like she was a spoiled grandkid.

"How was a small town like Bayport able to get such a big-name architect involved with the aquarium?" asked the dad of the boy in the Captain Hook shirt.

"Along with being a world-famous architect, Mr. V is a huge sea-life enthusiast. He jumped at the chance to build such an ambitious, groundbreaking exhibit," I told the adults. "He was so passionate about the project that he even footed part of the bill."

The father nodded, impressed. That was another great thing about Predator Reef—the parents were just as excited as the kids.

And now for the big moment when it would be revealed to the world.

"Are you ready to see Predator Reef?!" I asked the tour group. The kids all cheered and the parents clapped.

They weren't the only ones. TV cameras were rolling as visitors packed into the aquarium by the hundreds, crowding the lobby level to catch their first look at the spectacular new exhibit.

Mr. V beamed with pride as he took the microphone in front of the curtain, looking sharp in a captain's blazer embroidered with the aquarium's logo. The crowd gave him a warm round of applause as he got ready to speak. Mr. V had only recently moved to Bayport, but he'd already become a very popular public figure. He was such a nice guy and so enthusiastic about the aquarium that he was kind of like a cross between a grown-up kid and everyone's favorite uncle: You couldn't help but like him.

"Greetings, Bayport," he said in a strong New England accent that made the word "Bayport" sound more like "Baypaat."

New England wasn't really all that far from Bayport in terms of miles, but the strange non-rhotic accent with its drawn-out syllables and dropped *R*s (that's pretty much what non-rhotic means) was kind of funny and foreign-sounding to the ears of us Bayport High kids.

"As a child idolizing the great French sea explorer Jacques Cousteau, I developed a deep love of the ocean and all its many wonderful creatures," he told the crowd. "I have been lucky in my career to get to build many different kinds of architectural projects all over the world, but none of them are closer to my heart than Bayport Aquarium's Predator Reef. It's been a lifelong dream to use my architectural talents in a way that allows me to share my passion for the sea with the rest of the world—and I couldn't be happier with the result. I hope you all enjoy it as much as I do."

Applause turned to cheers as he cut the ribbon with an oversize pair of scissors. The big blue curtain swept aside, revealing Mr. V's fantastic seascape.

But something was wrong.

The crowd oohed and aahed at the swirl of colorful fish

and patrolling reef sharks, but I could tell something was off. From the nervous glances I saw Mr. V giving a couple of the staff members, I knew they sensed it too.

The animals seemed agitated, and the normally crystal clear water was stirred up and murky from all the activity. The blacktips were zipping back and forth instead of slowly cruising around the tank in their usual mellow glide. One of the larger zebra sharks was swimming in tight circles, whipping the surface with its long tail. And a lot of the smaller fish were clinging closely to the coral or hiding away in its many nooks and crannies.

There were BAD divers in the tank too, but that shouldn't have bothered the fish. The fish in Predator Reef were conditioned to pretty much ignore the divers when they weren't being fed, in which case they flocked to them like pigeons at the park. Even the predatory blacktip reef sharks were trained not to pay the divers any mind.

But it wasn't the animals we could see that had me worried. It was the one we couldn't.

The crowd could sense the staff's distress and started murmuring.

"Where's the turtle, Mommy?" one little girl asked.

Just then a dark shape began to swim up from the deepest part of the tank. Everyone peered down into the water expectantly.

"Is that Captain Hook?" another little kid asked, pointing at the figure.

It wasn't. It was one of the divers. Joe's dive instructor Aly swam to the surface and pulled off her mask. She looked frantic.

"She's gone!" she cried. "Captain Hook is gone!"

In her hand, Aly held a piece of broken coral smeared with what looked like blood.

DEEP-SEA DETECTIVES

3

JOE

PREDATOR REEF WAS MISSING ITS STAR attraction.

When Aly broke the surface holding the gory coral and told everyone that Captain Hook was gone, it sent the place into chaos. The crowd was horrified, the aquarium staff went into crisis mode, the news reporters started shouting questions, and some of the little kids started crying.

I was standing off to the side with some of my diving classmates when it happened. Frank turned around and shot me a look from his spot in the front row. I nodded. If Captain Hook really was missing—and I wasn't ready to concede that a five-hundred-pound giant turtle had just vanished without a trace—we were going to do everything we could to help find her. I knew how important the aquarium was to Frank.

When I got to the front, Frank was huddled with Aly and some of the other aquarium staff. I peered over the glass rail into the tank and took in the exhibit while I waited for them to finish. The water was kind of hazy from all the sand kicked up by the fish and divers, but the exhibit was still breathtaking. All the different colors and shapes amid the movement of the animals were almost hypnotic. I could see why Frank got so into this stuff.

Some of the BAD divers were still swimming around the tank, searching for any sign of what had happened to Captain Hook. How do you lose a giant sea turtle? I shook my head. I couldn't make sense of it.

I scoped out the rest of the lobby. Off to the side of the reef tank there was some kind of hydraulic lift, a robotic-looking piece of equipment with a small platform for raising and lowering heavy objects. What really grabbed my attention, though, was what was circling Predator Reef.

The entire lobby was surrounded by Shark Row, the huge doughnut-shaped tank where they kept the really big sharks. I didn't know what kind of sharks they were, but some of them were monstrous, as long as ten feet or even more, easily big enough to gobble up the little three-foot blacktip reef sharks in Predator Reef whole. The fact that they were slowly circling with grinning jaws full of jagged teeth made the whole scene extra sinister. It was enough to give you chills.

Frank shook my attention from the sharks as he and Aly briefed me on what they knew.

"Nobody has a clue what happened or when she might have disappeared," Frank said.

"No one saw her when the trainers fed the sharks this morning, but that's not so unusual," Aly explained. "Captain Hook is a late sleeper and will sometimes stay in her favorite nook until it's her turn for breakfast."

"So nobody was alarmed when they didn't see her," Frank said, picking up where Aly left off. "They had planned to feed her right after they cut the ribbon, so everybody could get a look."

"That's when we realized she was gone," Aly said. She paused before adding, "The nook is where I found the broken piece of coral."

"The red stuff on it . . . is it blood?" I asked after a second, not sure I really wanted to know the answer.

Aly hesitated. "That's what it looked like."

"They won't know for sure until they test it," Frank said. "We think someone took her, Joe. Five-hundred-pound turtles don't just disappear."

"The security cameras catch anything?" I asked.

"They're checking, but you don't just pick up a giant sea turtle, put it in your pocket, and walk out of the aquarium without anyone noticing," Frank said.

"Just getting her safely in and out of the exhibit requires a small hydraulic lift." Aly pointed to the piece of equipment

I'd seen off to the side of the exhibit just as her phone buzzed with a text.

"They're fast-forwarding through the security footage, but nothing so far," she reported. "It doesn't look like anyone who wasn't supposed to came or went through any of the aquarium exits after hours."

Her phone buzzed with another text.

"Gotta go," she said. "Emergency meeting."

Aly ran off to the side of the exhibit where Carter and the other BAD divers had assembled. When Carter saw she'd been talking to me, he tried to stare me down again. I just ignored him. Now wasn't the time to sweat some petty beef.

"What about underwater cameras?" I asked Frank. "They were going to launch a Turtle Cam, right?" The Turtle Cam, a twenty-four-hour webcam broadcast on the aquarium's website, had been a big part of the Predator Reef marketing push.

"They're checking that, too, but the exhibit is supposed to simulate the natural light cycle of a real tropical reef environment, so the lights don't come on until later in the morning. Anything that happened before that would just show up as dark shadows."

"But even if something did show up on the underwater cameras, the thieves still would have had to get her out of the tank without being seen by the aquarium's security cameras," I added, baffled by the lack of clues. "They must have left some kind of trail, right? It's not like she spontaneously combusted . . . and I know she wasn't abducted by aliens."

This was starting to look like one very big magic trick. Maybe we'd have better luck if we tried to figure out who the magician might be instead of how he or she did it.

"So who would have reason to take her?" I asked Frank.

"None of your business, that's who."

Unfortunately, it wasn't Frank who answered. It was Chief Olaf, Bayport's top cop. The chief tends to frown on our amateur detective work, even if we do often get better results than the professionals. I think it bugs him that a couple of unlicensed teenage investigators have just as impressive a crime-stopping track record as he does.

"This is a police matter, boys. I don't want you meddling," he said, fixing us with his patented stern glare. The chief likes to play the bad cop with us, but he's actually a pretty nice guy. For all the times he's threatened to have us arrested, he's never actually hauled us in. At least not yet.

"Besides, I think we've got our prime suspects right here," Chief Olaf pointed to the black-tipped shark fins slicing through the surface of Predator Reef. "I've watched enough *Shark Week* on TV to know a pack of aquatic killers when I see one."

"I don't think so, Chief," Frank said. "The sharks in the exhibit are too small to attack a large sea turtle like Captain Hook."

Judging from the annoyed look on his face, I don't think

the chief appreciated the marine biology lesson.

"Humph," the chief grunted, motioning toward the sharks. "If all two dozen of those things ganged up on it, that turtle wouldn't stand a chance."

"The blacktips may be social pack hunters, but they still wouldn't bother with prey that big. Even if they did, they wouldn't be able to eat Captain Hook's shell, so there would be evidence left behind." Frank went on schooling the chief despite the daggers he was shooting Frank's way. I swear, for someone so smart, my brother can be pretty dense sometimes. "You could maybe make the case that one of the big guys in Shark Row did it, but they're kept in a separate tank, and even the ten-foot sand tiger sharks wouldn't normally try to eat a five-hundred-pound turtle. Biologists think the great white that took a chunk out of Captain Hook's fin was at least a twenty-footer."

"Frank, why don't you worry about your job and let me do mine?" snapped the chief.

"Young Mr. Hardy is right, Chief," a voice said from behind us. Bradley Valledor walked up and put his hand on Frank's shoulder. "Our blacktips are too small and too well trained to have attacked Captain Hook."

Chief Olaf sighed. "You sure about that, Mr. Valledor? It would be the most obvious explanation, and in my experience the most obvious suspect is usually the culprit."

"Not this time, I'm afraid. It wasn't sharks that got Captain Hook. Someone stole her."

I could tell the chief didn't like that. If Mr. V was right, his job had just gotten a lot harder.

"Okay then, tell me what you think happened," he said to Mr. V. Chief Olaf turned to us. "If you boys would excuse us, I have official police business I need to discuss with Mr. Valledor."

"Actually, I'd prefer it if Frank and his brother stayed," Mr. V said.

"I'm sorry, come again?" Chief Olaf said, putting his hand to his ear like he'd misheard.

"Chief, you and your detectives will have full access to the aquarium and our staff—"

"Thank you, Mr. Valledor, but I don't see what that—" the chief began.

"And so will the Hardys."

"Now wait a second. I can't have a couple of kids running around interfering with our investigation."

"I don't give much credence to age, Chief," Mr. V said. "I wasn't any older than these young men are now when I designed my first building. I've heard that the Hardy boys are quite well regarded around Bayport for their investigative skills, and I intend to use every resource at our disposal to make sure Captain Hook is returned to us safely."

"Fine," the chief conceded, turning to Frank and me. "But you two steer clear of the crime scene until my team is finished. I'm going to have to interview the entire aquarium staff as well as anyone else who had access to the exhibit, and I don't want to catch you saying as much as a syllable to any of my witnesses until I've talked to them first, got it?"

"Yes, sir!" we both said, barely able to contain our excitement over the free investigative pass Mr. V had just given us. We usually had to sneak around behind the chief's back to solve a mystery.

I think we might have seemed a little too excited about it for the chief's liking.

"You do anything on this case without getting my permission first and I'll slap the cuffs on you myself," he warned.

A man in a slick business suit tapped Mr. V on the shoulder. A tall young woman in an equally nice suit stood by his side.

"Excuse me, Bradley. The press is ready to take your statement whenever you are," the man said in a New England accent that was even thicker than Mr. V's.

"Thank you, Ron. I'll be there momentarily," Mr. V said, and turned to the chief. "Chief Olaf, this is my firm's PR director, Ron Burris, and my assistant, Laura. I've already instructed them to make all of the firm's resources available to assist with the investigation. Now, Ron, if you would, please draft an international press release offering a one-million-dollar reward for information leading directly to Captain Hook's safe return and forward it to Laura for my approval."

Ron Burris's face twisted up like he had just been slapped silly. "But sir, that's crazy, you can't just—"

"That will be all, Ron," Mr. V cut him off dismissively. "Please tell the press I'm ready."

Mr. V left his PR director in stunned silence and marched over to the news cameras with Laura following close behind. Frank and I watched as Mr. V announced the impressive reward and made an impassioned plea for help finding Captain Hook. It wasn't until he addressed the "kidnappers" directly that we realized just how bad the situation was.

"If someone out there took our beloved turtle, please, I beg you, bring her back before it's too late. Captain Hook requires special medication to be administered daily. Without it . . ." Mr. V's voice started to shake.

He took a minute to collect himself, then looked directly into the camera, his gaze intensifying.

"Whoever you are, you have served that turtle with a death warrant."

DEADLY MEDICINE

4

FRANK

MR. V'S WORDS ECHOED IN MY HEAD. Captain Hook was in grave danger. I knew the vets kept a close eye on her, but I hadn't realized how serious her condition truly was. We had to find her, and fast.

There was one major problem. Usually when I'm on a case I have a hunch about where to begin. Not this time.

Mr. V walked out of the aquarium with his head down and made his way to the Rolls-Royce parked right in front. A tall tuxedoed chauffeur who reminded me of Alfred from the Batman comics opened the back door for Mr. V and Laura. They drove off with the news cameras still rolling, leaving Ron behind to handle the reporters.

With Mr. V gone, most of the cameramen turned their

attention to a group of protesters from the Bayport Animal Liberation Force (aka BALF) waving signs in front of the aquarium and chanting, "Free the fish! Free the fish!"

One girl had a sign with a drawing of a turtle behind bars wearing a prison jumpsuit. When she spotted me in my Bayport Aquarium staff shirt, she screamed in my direction.

"How would you like it if someone locked you in a cage and exploited you for commercial gain, huh?!"

I should have ignored her, but I couldn't just stand by and listen to her and her BALF friends bad-mouth the aquarium without all the facts. I thought maybe if they knew more about how the aquarium really operates, they might be more open-minded about things, so I went over to talk to her.

"Excuse me, but I think you have it all wrong," I said. "Bayport Aquarium does more to raise awareness for endangered species protection than just about anyone. The aquarium takes great care of its animals. They saved Captain Hook's life! They aren't exploiting her. She's a symbol of hope for the whole local conservation movement."

"Turtle torturer!" the girl yelled. It was like she didn't even hear me.

"Forget them, kid," Ron Burris said, pulling me aside. "Types like that, they won't see any opinion but their own."

Ron was right. Sure, I understand some of the arguments against keeping wild animals in captivity, but in the case of a top-notch aquarium like Bayport's, the pros clearly outweighed the cons. BALF wasn't going to see that, though. They believed that it was wrong to put animals in captivity for any reason, regardless of the potential benefits to the animal or environmental causes.

"I only have a minute, but I wanted to see if you have any theories yet about the turtle situation," Ron said, talking quickly as we moved away from the protesters. "You think those crazies could have had something to do with it?"

"It's too early to speculate," I said, making a mental note to add BALF to my list. "We're just starting to gather information."

Ron handed me his card. "You give me a call as soon as you get any leads. Mr. Valledor is going to want regular reports."

"No problem, we—"

Ron's phone chimed before I could finish my answer.

"Excuse me." Ron held up a finger as he checked the caller ID. "I'm sorry, I have to take this. You boys keep up the good work."

A second later he was headed in the opposite direction with the phone up to his ear.

"This is Ron. . . . That's right, we want to do the entire office in oak and leather, very executive and classy. . . . Yes, you can quote me on that. . . . No, that's Burris, B-U-R-R-I-S," I overheard him say as he walked away. With his accent, the way he said "R-R" sounded more like "Ah-Ah."

I thought it was a little rude of him to be worrying about

another client's office decor at a time like this, but I figured Mr. V's people still had a business to run even during a crisis.

Joe came over to join me.

"Figures Eric the Ecoterrorist would be here."

Joe nodded in the direction of the dreadlocked guy at the front of the BALF protest holding the biggest sign and shouting the loudest.

The kid in question was a Bayport High student named Eric Frohman, whom everyone called Eric the Ecoterrorist. He had a reputation for taking activism to the extreme, protesting anything and everything to do with animals or the environment that might be considered the least bit controversial.

"You heard about the chimpanzee incident, right?" I asked my brother. "When he was arrested for trying to climb into the monkey house at the zoo to free the animals."

"Yeah," Joe said, laughing. "When the security guard caught up to him, he had his dreadlocks tangled in the fence and was trying to get unstuck while the chimps pelted him with their poo."

The story had been a big hit at Bayport High, and Eric wasn't likely to live it down anytime soon.

"Because he was a minor and didn't have a record, the judge told him the humiliation factor was punishment enough and let him go with probation," I said to Joe. "But it sure hasn't stopped him from protesting."

"And we know he's willing to break the law for his cause," Joe added. "He did it once. . . ."

"He might do it again," I finished the thought. "We're going to have to take a closer look at where Eric the Ecoterrorist was when Captain Hook disappeared and see if he or his crew knew anyone who could have helped him get into the aquarium."

I pulled out the case file notebook I carry with me and jotted down "Eric the Ecoterrorist" under the heading "Suspects."

When I looked up, I saw another familiar Bayport High face in the crowd.

"Hey, it's the Collector," Joe said, spotting him as well.

Murph "the Collector" Murphy got his nickname because that's what he does—he collects things. Lots of things. From comic books to vintage Japanese toy robots to dinosaur fossils, if it can be collected, there's a good chance he either collects it or knows a ton about it.

"If you're the president of the Bayport Nerds Association, then Murph Murphy is its chairman," Joe joked.

"You're just jealous because we're more enlightened than you," I said. "Simply because we like to be knowledgeable about a lot of different subjects doesn't automatically make us nerds."

"Sure it does, bro," Joe said. "But you have to admit, Murph really does have you beat when it comes to knowing obscure facts about random stuff."

Murph also had me beat in the wardrobe department. He was what you might call a nerd fashionista, combining classic geek style with a trendy *GQ* fashion sense.

"He's really rocking the aqua-hipster look today," Joe observed as Murph walked along the pier, sporting an ocean-blue blazer and matching bow tie dotted with tiny sharks.

"We've been seeing a lot of our man Murph since we started hanging out at the aquarium, huh?" Joe asked.

"He's a member," I told my brother. "He considers himself one of Bayport's foremost amateur aquarists, and from what I've seen, I'd have to agree with him."

"Is that a fancy way of saying he's a fish fanatic?" Joe asked.

"Pretty much. The guy really knows his fish. He had me over to his house to check out his new saltwater tank—it's one of the coolest I've ever seen outside of an actual aquarium."

"Looks like you guys just found your next case," Murph observed after catching my eye and heading over. "This is the biggest aquarium heist I've ever heard of. The online aquarist message boards must be crazy right now."

"You mean you've heard of other aquarium heists before? Like that's an actual thing?" Joe asked.

"Sure," Murph said. "There's a huge underground market for rare fish. Usually divers illegally smuggle them from reefs to sell for top dollar to private collectors, but every once in a while you hear about fish disappearing from aquariums, too. Typically the smaller fish go missing because they're less noticeable and easier to transport. A five-hundred-pound endangered turtle has to be a record!"

"Have you ever heard about fish heists around Bayport?" I asked.

"Nah," Murph started to reply before pausing for a second. "Well, come to think of it, maybe."

All four Hardy eyebrows shot up. Murph had our attention.

"There has been a lot of online chatter lately about someone local selling rare tropical fish, like some of the ones in the Predator Reef exhibit: clown triggerfish, yellow longnose butterfly fish, and emperor angelfish. There's even speculation that someone could be smuggling them from inside the aquarium. It's all just rumors, though; a lot of the stuff you hear online turns out to be bogus."

"Wouldn't the aquarium notice if someone was stealing their fish?" Joe asked.

"Maybe not," I jumped in before Murph could answer. "The aquarium imported thousands of specimens for the exhibit. And a certain number of fish die here just like they would in the wild, so the staff probably wouldn't be suspicious if a couple went missing. It's still a far cry from stealing a giant sea turtle, though."

"So how much would a collector pay for a giant sea turtle on the black market if someone did manage to steal it?" Joe followed up.

"A *lot*," Murph said. "Rare wildlife collectors are just as competitive as other kinds of collectors who pay crazy amounts for stuff. Some do really love animals and mean well, but they just take it to the extreme. The worst are the ones who see their aquariums as status symbols."

From the disgust on Murph's face, it was obvious what he thought about them.

"Those collectors don't actually care about the art of collecting something. They just want to show off their wealth. From what you hear, it's the same guys who shell out millions for stolen masterwork paintings and exotic blood diamonds who have the biggest collections of endangered wildlife. And the rarer the animal, the more they're willing to spend."

"So a famous endangered sea turtle like Captain Hook might be a nice addition for a big-time collector," Joe speculated.

Murph shook his head, a grim look on his face. "It gets worse, guys. It's not just collectors who could be after her. Turtle parts go for big bucks on the TCM market."

"TCM?" Joe asked.

"Traditional Chinese medicine," Murph clarified.

I took a deep breath. I knew where Murph was going with this, and I didn't like it.

"Some Eastern cultures use different animal parts in ancient homeopathic cures and superstition rituals," I explained. "It's a huge conservation problem. A lot of the global poaching that goes on is fueled by the demand for traditional medicines. It's one of the big reasons sea turtles are so endangered in the first place."

"Poaching?" Joe asked. "You mean like people killing animals illegally?"

"Yup," Murph said. "There's a black market for everything

from rhino horns to tiger claws to turtle shells. Just the shell of a sea turtle as big as Captain Hook could sell for hundreds of thousands. And a lot of the organs are used for different cures and as exotic delicacies."

I really didn't want to think about what that might mean for Captain Hook.

"But is that really a problem in the United States?" I asked. "The endangered species laws are so strict here that I thought most of the turtle poaching happened in foreign waters, where the laws aren't enforced."

"Exactly," Murph said. "The rarer something is, the more people are willing to spend. So who knows how much a live specimen from the United States might go for if you found the right buyer?"

Suddenly Mr. V's million-dollar reward didn't seem that outlandish. Someone might be willing to spend more than that just to add Captain Hook to their private collection . . . or much, much worse.

"And that's the other thing," Murph said hesitantly. "There's been chatter about something else. Word is there's a cell of TCM poachers operating off the Bayport coast."

Murph began to get this queasy look. When he started talking again, I found out why.

"They've been cutting the fins off sharks to sell for shark-fin soup," he said. "The mutilated bodies have been washing up on shore."

5 THE BRITISH ARE COMING

JOE

THE NEWS JUST KEPT GETTING WORSE. It was bad enough that Captain Hook needed special medication and that someone could have jeopardized her life by stealing her for their private collection. But the possibility that poachers wanted her for parts made me feel ill. I wasn't as emotionally attached to her as Frank or Mr. V, but Captain Hook was a beautiful living creature, and I was beyond bummed to think someone might want to chop her up and turn her into turtle tonic.

Murph wished us luck and promised to keep an ear out for any more intel on Captain Hook, stolen fish, or the poachers. The crowd around the aquarium was starting to thin out as the news vans dispersed in search of someone else to interview. That's when I saw a tall, slim man in a custom-tailored pinstripe suit hurrying along the pier away from the aquarium. Maybe it was the briefcase he was carrying, but something about him looked really familiar.

"Is that . . . ?"

"Dirk Bishop?" Frank finished my question before I had a chance.

"No way, dude. It can't be."

"I think it is."

"Well, let's find out."

Dirk Bishop was the one who got away, a snooty British treasure hunter who'd tried to buy some stolen gold coins we'd found aboard a Revolutionary War ship. Last time we'd seen him, he'd been on his way to make the buy, carrying what we thought was a briefcase full of cash, but he'd gotten spooked and took off before we could nab him. No one had heard a peep from Bishop since.

We'd figured he'd gone back to jolly old England. But here he was again, right back where we saw him last, rushing along the docks with a briefcase, looking all too sneaky. Bad juju followed Bishop around like an ugly puppy—all the people he'd done business with on our last case had ended up either dead, kidnapped, or in jail—so whatever had brought him back to Bayport was bound to be bad news.

"If it is him, he has real nerve showing his face in Bayport again," Frank muttered as we trailed the man along the pier.

"He must have known the police didn't have anything on him to risk another trip back here."

"Either that or something gave him a good enough reason to take the chance anyway," I said, wondering what kind of trouble he intended to stir up this time.

There was something else about Bishop too. The guy was seriously tied into the international black market—and his treasure-hunting résumé included extensive experience as a shipwreck salvage diver, searching old, abandoned ships for loot. Was it a coincidence that he showed up right after someone had stolen a living treasure from a four-hundred-thousand-gallon tank?

Frank and I kept our distance so Bishop wouldn't notice he was being tailed. He made his way to the water taxi stop at the end of the pier, where one of the pontoon boats was getting ready to shove off. It was the only one in sight, so Frank and I were going to have to make a decision.

"We can't tail him once he's on the water," Frank said, echoing my thoughts. "Do we give up and track him down later or let him know we're onto him?"

"I think our guest deserves a welcoming committee," I said.

We hopped aboard the water taxi just as it was about to take off. Bishop gave us a look like he recognized us but couldn't quite place who we were. A second later his eyes narrowed.

"Oh, it's you," he said in his proper British accent.

"Hey, Dirk," I said cheerily. "It's good to see you, too. Welcome back to Bayport."

"If it isn't America's own young Sherlock and Watson," he said, though he didn't make it sound like a compliment. "What an unpleasant surprise."

"We're surprised to see you, too, considering how things turned out the last time," Frank said.

"It turns out your little town isn't quite the worthless flotsam I had initially been led to believe," Bishop sniffed. "Bayport, it seems, offers quite a few, uh, shall we say, rather interesting aquatic attractions. Although I find many of its human residents leave something to be desired."

There was little mystery as to whom Bishop was talking about.

"Thirty-five hundred miles is a long way to travel just to see some fish," I said.

"Your aquarium is quite impressive, I must say. Mr. Valledor has outdone himself with that exhibit of his. It's close enough to the real thing to make even the most seasoned ocean enthusiast momentarily forget they're inside an aquarium. A shame, though. I had rather hoped to see the famous Captain Hook for myself."

"We bet you did," Frank retorted.

"I'm sorry, I don't have the slightest idea what you mean," Bishop said, looking annoyed.

"It's kind of strange that every time you show up in Bayport, something valuable goes missing," I said.

“Whatever it is that you’re insinuating, I resent the accusation. I am a legitimate businessman, and it is a strictly legitimate interest that brings me back to your town, though I’m now beginning to regret that decision,” he said with a sneer in our direction. “Whatever may have become of your turtle, I hope they find her. I’ve spent quite a bit of time below the surface of our fair seas, and I’ve come to believe that the lives of our finned and flippered friends are often more precious than many of the human beings I’ve had the displeasure of meeting.”

Before we could reply, he signaled for the water taxi driver to stop.

“Now if you’ll excuse me,” he said as he stood up and brushed the wrinkles from his suit. “Cabbie, you can stop here. I usually find boat rides quite relaxing, but something on this one seems to have made me seasick. Good day.” He cleared his throat like he had a nasty glob of snot stuck there before adding, “Gentlemen.”

“I don’t think that dude likes us too much,” I said to my brother.

“Well, the feeling’s mutual,” Frank said.

Bishop had obviously gotten off short of his final destination, so wherever he had intended to go would have to remain a mystery for now. Letting him know we were onto him had been a calculated risk. Some criminals get jumpy when they know you’re onto them; they get sloppy or force their hands, unintentionally exposing themselves or their accomplices. Others keep their cool and just grow more cautious or lie low until the heat dies down. I had a feeling Bishop wasn't the type to scare easily.

"Maybe giving up the element of surprise wasn't the best idea after all," I said to my brother as Bishop walked off, clutching his briefcase.

"If he's involved, whatever's in that briefcase could be crucial to solving the crime," Frank said.

I watched Bishop and the briefcase disappear around the corner. "Hopefully we didn't just blow our only chance to find out."

6 SHARK!

FRANK

JOE AND I WENT FROM ONE TYPE OF shark encounter to another. Bishop may not have had a dorsal fin, but he was just as dangerous. The zebra sharks and blacktips we were going to be diving with at the aquarium were cuddly water bunnies compared to old Dirk.

Right after our watery run-in with Mr. Bishop, we'd received a call from Ron Burris saying Chief Olaf's forensic divers were done in the reef exhibit. They hadn't turned up any new evidence, so now it was our turn to investigate Predator Reef.

We met Ron in front of the aquarium. He was still in his fancy suit, but his tie was loosened at the collar, and it looked like he'd been doing a lot of running around since we'd last seen him.

"Let's walk and talk, guys," he said, leading the way inside toward Predator Reef, speaking rapid-fire the whole way. "I don't have much time. The firm already had a zillion things going on, and this whole missing turtle business has blown my schedule to pieces. A disaster like that at an exhibit we designed is a public-relations nightmare. Not that it's anything I can't handle."

Ron kept on talking as we approached the exhibit.

"I don't know what you two did to the police chief, by the way, but he wasn't very happy when he called to let us know it was your turn to take a dip into the exhibit. Don't worry, though, we've got your backs. Mr. Valledor says to tell you that you have our absolute support in this investigation. He's got his hands full today, so he wants you to call me with a detailed report as soon as you're out of the water."

With his accent, "water" came out "wataah." But with his confident demeanor and ability to talk, I could totally see how he'd make a good PR guy. He'd been public relating so fast, we hadn't been able to get a word in.

"Did the police find anything at all?" I blurted before Ron could utter another sentence.

"Nah, nada. Nothing they told us about anyway. As of now, they don't know any more than we do. What about you boys? What have the detectives detected?" he asked, flipping the question back to us.

"Nothing solid yet," I said cautiously. Sure, we'd ID'ed a couple of suspects in Eric the Ecoterrorist and Bishop, and we had Murph's tip about the poachers, but it didn't help to go broadcasting your hunches this early in an investigation.

"Come on, you can do better than that," Ron said. "Give me something I can take back to Mr. Valledor."

"We're investigating a couple of possible leads not directly linked to the aquarium," Joe said, giving Ron just a little taste of what we'd found. "We'll be able to give you details as soon as we know more."

"Not connected to the aquarium, huh?" He nodded. "Okay, okay, that's a start. It'll have to do for now at least."

Ron handed Joe his card, so now we each had one. "I've got to get on over to see Mr. Valledor, but call me the second you know something. And if you need anything at all, just tell me and I'll make sure we get it for you."

By the time we opened our mouths to thank him, he was already on his way out of the room. He turned back before reaching the door.

"Be careful in there," he said, pointing at the circling blacktips. "Mr. V is counting on you."

Okay, so diving with sharks may sound like a really bad idea, but in reality there wasn't much to fear from the sharks in the exhibit. Zebra sharks mostly eat crustaceans, mollusks, and small fish. There has never been a reported zebra attack on humans. At the aquarium, they were fed by hand.

The blacktips were a slightly different story, however. They look totally sharklike and can be dangerous if you're diving with them in the wild.

"Frank, did you know that unlike most sharks, the blacktips live in social groups?" Joe asked me a little too loudly, trying to show off for Aly, who was walking past with another BAD diver. "You may not know this, but the staff has actually trained the ones at the aquarium to eat together at feeding stations so they won't munch on the smaller fish in the exhibit. A well-fed shark is a happy shark. The blacktips in Predator Reef are so well conditioned to humans, they usually just go about their business as if the divers are any other kind of non-prey fish."

All I could do was shake my head and try not to laugh. My brother was repeating the same exact facts I'd told him that morning. He was laying it on thick for Aly. I snuck a peek over at Aly and saw her give a little smirk in Joe's direction while pretending not to notice him showing off for her.

A minute later she walked over with the other diver, a guy everyone called Big Chuck. Big Chuck worked with Aly teaching the scuba classes (and just in case it wasn't obvious from the nickname, Chuck was not a small dude). Big Chuck was wearing a big wet suit, and Aly had on a Bayport Aquarium hoodie.

"Oh hi, Aly, I didn't see you there," Joe hammed it up for his crush. "I was just telling my brother about some of the sharks in the exhibit, right, Frank?"

"Mm-hmm," I said, biting my tongue to keep from laughing. I hoped Aly didn't notice.

"Okay, Aquaman," she said to Joe with a knowing smile.

"I've got to take care of some stuff so I can't hang around, but Big Chuck is going to be supervising the dive to make sure everything goes smoothly."

"We'll be fine," Joe said. "I'm practically a pro."

"Not yet you're not. You still have your big certification test coming up tomorrow," she reminded him.

"I've got it in the bag," Joe bragged. "I think the instructor likes me."

Aly laughed and turned to Big Chuck. "Take good care of them, Chuck. It will make me look bad if Joe drowns before passing the exam."

Joe's confidence drained away as soon as Aly walked off. Something else had grabbed his attention.

"Um, hey, Frank," Joe whispered, making sure Aly didn't accidentally overhear. "We don't have to worry about them when we dive, do we?"

He pointed to the Shark Row tank, where the big sharks slowly circled the aquarium lobby. It wasn't crazy of him to be nervous. While the vicious-looking sand tigers were actually (usually) pretty docile around divers unless provoked or threatened, they were still fearsome predators. The aquarium staff took every precaution to make sure there were never any incidents.

"Nothing to worry about," I reassured him. "All the big ones stay in Shark Row. There aren't any sand tigers in Predator Reef. The exhibits share a holding tank where animals can be moved for veterinary care, but it's always kept sealed off from one side. That way the big sharks can't ever get into the reef exhibit, where they might be tempted to feed on their smaller cousins."

"Ugh, they're cannibals?" Joe grimaced. "As if they weren't scary enough."

"They're a lot more likely to eat each other than people," I said, taking the chance to give my brother a better understanding of sharks. "Statistically, more people are killed every year by cows than by sharks. People are afraid of sharks, but the truth is that sharks have a whole lot more to fear from us. Shark hunting, commercial fishing, and the illegal shark-fin trade have decimated global shark populations to critical levels."

Joe rolled his eyes. "That's great to know, bro, but it's the Joe Hardy population I'm worried about."

"Even if we were diving with larger species, few shark attacks on humans are ever fatal," I told him. "Most are just cases of mistaken identity, where the shark confuses the person for a seal or other natural prey animal. You don't have much meat on your bones anyway, so even if one did accidentally take a bite out of you, they'd probably just spit you out like a bad brussels sprout."

"Well, that's reassuring," Joe huffed.

I was disturbed too, but not because I was worried about a shark attack. There was another reason I had the shark-hunting problem on my mind as we geared up to dive into Predator Reef.

Like Murph had said, sharks are an essential ingredient in a lot of traditional Chinese medicines.

Just like with sea turtles.

As we entered the calm water of Predator Reef, I hoped we would find something to prove that wasn't the case with Captain Hook.

Since Joe was taking scuba lessons and had a lot more experience than I did, I was going to let him go first and do most of the dive detecting in the deeper part of the exhibit tank, while I searched closer to the surface. We were going to use the aquarium's special "dive comm" masks, which would allow us to communicate with each other underwater, so we could actually talk without having to rely only on hand signals.

A rainbow of brightly colored fish scattered in front of him as Joe began his descent.

"How's it looking down there, Joe?" I asked. The dive comm masks made everything sound a bit bubbly, kind of like you might expect someone to sound underwater.

"Totally sweet! It's like exploring a whole different planet!" Joe's enthusiasm was obvious even through the sound of all the bubbles. And there were lots of bubbles. They spewed upward toward the surface as he talked, making it a little difficult to clearly see Joe as he dived down.

I swam through the shallows above Joe. I didn't have the clear view he did because of the bubbles, but it really was beautiful. Actually being underwater in the fishes' world was unlike anything I'd ever seen before.

"I'm going to head for the nook where they found the broken coral," Joe said, releasing another stream of air bubbles from the dive comm mask.

"Right behind you," I replied.

A series of sleek, shark-shaped shadows passed over the bottom of the reef as the blacktips patrolled their domain. Man, was this cool! A moment later the cloud of fish vanished in a flash, taking cover in the coral. That was strange. The fish shouldn't have been scared of us. It took me a second to realize it wasn't us they were afraid of. Another shadow had appeared. It might have seemed cool too, if it wasn't so terrifying. It was shaped like a shark as well, but this one was huge. Like, horror-movie huge. I wiped my mask, thinking maybe the condensation was making me see things. It wasn't.

Predator Reef had an uninvited visitor. One of the big sand tiger sharks had somehow gotten into the exhibit.

It wasn't just any sand tiger either. From the size of it, it could only be Bruce, the biggest shark in the whole aquarium. And Bruce did not look like a happy shark.

Bruce wasn't as large as a great white, but he was still *big*. Ten feet long and over four hundred pounds, with a mouthful of hideous needle-sharp daggers meant for spearing his prey, he looked like a swimming nightmare.

I shook my head in disbelief. He shouldn't have been in the reef tank with us. And whoever had let him out of Shark Row had him very riled up. He swam around Joe in big circles the way sharks sometimes do when they're stalking prey. With each pass the circle would get smaller until the shark was within easy striking distance.

Joe hadn't seen him yet. But he had stopped swimming, and I could tell he sensed something was wrong.

"Hey, bro, where'd all the fish go? Is something going on up there?" Joe asked. "It's hard to see through all the bubbles."

"Shark!" I yelled. "We have to get out of the tank!"

"Duh, there are about thirty of them. Stop messing with me," he said.

"I'm not messing with you, Joe!" I pleaded. "Get out of there now! One of the sand tigers got into the tank!"

"Ha, ha, very funn—" Joe started to say. Then he saw Bruce. "Oh boy."

I saw a stream of bubbles spew from Joe's mask and hit Bruce in his snout as he circled. Sharks have sensory organs in their noses that can pick up the tiniest electrical impulses in the water. To the shark, the unexpected burst of bubbles must have felt like an all-out assault!

Bruce whipped around and charged into the bubbles, filling the space between Joe and me. I was still a few feet above Joe, and I swam hard for the surface as the giant shark passed close enough that I felt the water from his wake punch me in the legs. Then something clamped onto my arm from above.

Oh no!

But it wasn't the shark; it was Big Chuck pulling me out of the water to safety. Luckily, I'd only been in a few feet of water, where he could reach me. Joe was still down there, though.

My heart was pumping like a piston inside my chest and my head was throbbing from the quick ascent, but I couldn't worry about that now. Not while my brother was still underwater with the shark.

"Joe!" I yelled into the dive comm mask. "Take cover in the coral nook!"

Joe didn't respond.

"Joe!" I yelled again, but there wasn't any answer.

I tried to dive back into the tank after him, but Big Chuck wrapped his beefy arms around me and wouldn't let go.

I looked down helplessly.

The water was all cloudy with sand and bubbles. Deep below I could make out the form of the thrashing shark. There was no sign of Joe. Not until a second later. That's when his scuba mask floated to the surface.

7 LIVE BAIT

JOE

I GOTTA SAY, DIVING IN THE REEF WAS DEFInitely one of the awesomest things I had ever experienced. Or at least it was until Bruce showed up.

One second I was swimming through masses of amazing colorful fish and the next I was all alone. I was trying to figure out where all the fish went when someone dimmed the lights in the tank. That's what it looked like at least. I thought Frank was playing with me when he said one of the sand tigers had gotten into the reef exhibit. It wasn't until I started to make out the shape of the massive shadow passing over me that I realized what was going on. I had just turned into shark bait.

Even with the bubbles clouding my vision, there was no mistaking the ferocious shark circling above me.

"Oh boy," I said, and actually laughed. It was an odd thing to do the moment before a shark tries to eat you, but I couldn't help thinking about Aly jokingly calling me Aquaman. The laugh didn't last long as it hit me that I might never get to see Aly again.

Then the bubbles from my dive comm mask hit Bruce in his ugly snoot. He didn't seem to like that one bit. The shark charged. I could just make out Frank above me, swimming frantically for the surface. I wanted to follow, but the shark was between us, cutting off my escape. I was trapped between an angry shark and the bottom of the tank.

I swam for the closest coral formation, hoping to find somewhere to hide. The shark passed just over my head like a torpedo, its huge jaws chomping down on a mouthful of water. I heard Frank over the dive comm mask telling me to head for Captain Hook's nook. Unfortunately, Bruce got there first. I found myself looking right into a grinning mouth chock-full of razor-sharp teeth.

Bruce charged toward me. I felt like the little clown fish being chased around by the shark in *Finding Nemo*. It was a lot more fun to watch on the screen, I can tell you that!

I swam for my life, diving behind an outcrop of coral on the floor of the exhibit just as the shark slammed into it, shattering the coral to bits. The shark's tail whipped past my head as it swung around for another charge. There was nowhere left for me to go.

That's when I noticed something strange on the floor of

the tank under where the coral had been. It looked kind of like a trapdoor. With Bruce barreling straight at me, I didn't have a lot of time to think about it. I reached for the small metal ring mounted on the door and pulled.

The door swung open, creating a suction effect kind of like the drain plug being pulled on a big bathtub. I slipped through in a rush of water and slid the door closed behind me just as the shark's jaws snapped shut on the place where my head had been.

I was temporarily safe from the shark, but somehow my predicament had gone from bad to worse. My regulator had torn out of my mouth during my escape! No regulator meant no air. *Don't panic, dude.* I tried to follow the emergency procedures Aly had taught me and did my best to hold my breath and stay calm until I could assess my situation.

I was in a small airtight holding tank, just big enough for a diver.

A diver and maybe a five-hundred-pound turtle.

Had I just discovered how someone stole Captain Hook? If I was lucky, I'd get the chance to contemplate it later. Right then I had a more urgent mystery to solve—namely, how I was going to get out of the holding tank without drowning. I couldn't hold my breath for much longer. I reached behind me for my Octopus—that's the backup regulator attached to the scuba tank—but the hose was caught in the trapdoor. I couldn't get it free without opening the hatch and exposing myself to Bruce.

Just then I saw another latch, this one on the bottom of the tank. My lungs throbbed and my eyeballs felt like they were going to bulge out of my head. Out of options and nearly out of air, I grabbed the latch and yanked. The water trapped in the holding tank dumped out all at once as I fell through the air into total darkness.

8 OF SHARKS AND MEN

FRANK

JOE HAD VANISHED. JUST LIKE CAPTAIN Hook.

I struggled against Big Chuck, trying to get loose so I could dive back into the water after my brother. I broke free, but before I could leap into the tank, Chuck yanked away my regulator and tossed it aside. I wasn't going anywhere without that no matter how much I wanted to.

"I'm sorry, man," Chuck said. "I can't let you go down there. Not until we get the vets to tranquilize that shark."

I stared down, looking for some sign that Joe was okay. There wasn't any blood in the water, and I could only hope that meant my brother had somehow managed to escape the shark's bite without drowning. But where had he gone?

Bruce looked as confused as I was. I could see him circling along the bottom of the tank, searching for his prey. When I reached down to pick up my brother's scuba mask, I saw a face reflected in the water—one that wasn't mine. I looked up. A hooded figure leaned over the rail one level above, watching me. As soon as the person realized I'd seen them, they bolted.

Innocent people usually don't run away.

"Get help for my brother!" I called to Big Chuck as I took off after the suspect, kicking off my fins and dropping my air tank as I ran. Luckily, we had been wearing dive boots under our fins to protect our feet from the sharp coral. I never would have been able to give chase in bare feet.

The figure ran down an escalator in the wrong direction, leaping the final few feet to the first floor and sprinting for the main exit. He or she was wearing a Bayport Aquarium hoodie, but I couldn't see their face. My only hope was to catch them. The figure fled through the aquarium exit and I followed in close pursuit, chasing him or her along the pier toward the harbor.

The suspect ran toward the boat rental place next to the water taxi station and leaped from the dock. For a second I thought they were going to dive into the bay, but they landed on the bow of one of the little motorboats tourists rent to tootle around the harbor. The kid running the rental booth yelled for them to stop, but the suspect already had the motor running and a second later was pulling away from the dock. Luckily, the little boats weren't built for speed. There was a water taxi nearby, and I managed to hop aboard just before it shoved off.

"Follow that boat!" I said to the elderly driver. He gave me a funny look, but he did as I asked. I don't think he'd gotten that request before.

The perp's escape boat may not have been very fast, but neither was my water taxi. You know those high-speed car chases they show on the news? Well, this was the low-speed boat version.

"Can't you step on it?!" I asked the driver.

"What do you think this is, a James Bond movie?" The driver laughed. "We're in a water taxi pontoon, not a speedboat."

The driver was right, but the perp was getting away and there was no way we were going to catch up to them in the water taxi. The driver's James Bond comment did give me an idea, though. When in doubt, ask yourself, What would 007 do?

I saw my chance when the little motorboat veered back toward us to avoid hitting a terrified paddleboater. It was just close enough for me to try something drastic. I gave a running start and leaped from the water taxi with everything I had.

And landed in the water with an unheroic splash a few feet short of the motorboat. The wake from the little boat smacked me in the face as the perp got away.

The water taxi driver was in stitches when he circled back to pick me up.

"Your fare is on me, son," he said when he finally managed to stop laughing. "That's the most entertainment I've had on the job in a long time."

I watched the hooded figure recede into the bay until the little boat disappeared around the bend of the harbor past the old industrial docks. Was it the same person who had stolen Captain Hook? Whoever they were, if they had intentionally released Bruce into Predator Reef while Joe and I were diving, then they were guilty of attempted murder. At least I hoped it was only attempted. I still didn't know if Joe had managed to somehow make it out of the tank alive.

He must have, right? That's what I kept telling myself. If the big sand tiger shark had gotten him, there would have been blood in the water. I shuddered. He was probably hiding somewhere in the coral until it was safe to swim to the surface. He would have had plenty of air in his tank. Or maybe he made it to the surface in a different part of the reef where I couldn't see him. Unless he'd gotten stuck somewhere in the coral out of Bruce's reach . . .

Stop it, Frank! Joe is going to be okay. He has to be.

9

UNDER THE SEA

JOE

THOSE FEW SECONDS AFTER I PULLED the latch on the second trapdoor were terrifying. I wasn't airborne for long, but it felt like I was falling through the bottom of the world. I landed with a soggy thump a moment later. All I could see was total blackness. This must be what being blind feels like.

I quickly checked for any scrapes, cuts, or broken bones. Nope, just sore from the fall. I tried to keep calm and use my other senses to get my bearings. I could hear the muffled burble of the four hundred thousand gallons of water in the reef tank somewhere above me, and I caught a noseful of an old musty smell. Like ancient journey-to-the-center-of-the-earth old.

That's kind of what it felt like too—like I'd fallen straight through the earth into a dark underworld. At least I was alive. The dark was really starting to creep me out, though. Had I escaped from the jaws of a killer shark only to face some new horror I couldn't even see? I fumbled around until I found the dive light that was hooked to my wet suit and clicked it on. The little beam felt like a breath of fresh air for my eyes after being surrounded by all that inky nothingness. Yes! Let there be light! But where was I?

Turns out I was in a really old tunnel. The floors and walls were packed dirt reinforced by wood beams. Or, to be more precise, rotting wood beams. There were old tracks running along the floor. I shone the light back up at the trapdoor. Beside it there was a small hydraulic lift similar to the one next to Predator Reef.

Everything started to click into place.

So that was how Captain Hook had vanished—through the trapdoor hidden under the coral on the bottom of the reef exhibit, into the secret holding tank, onto the hydraulic lift, and into the underground tunnel I found myself in now. The tunnel totally explained how someone could have entered Predator Reef and abducted Captain Hook without being caught on camera. A diver could have swum up from below and never even had to poke their head out of the water.

I examined the holding tank with my flashlight. It was a brilliant piece of engineering. It was airtight, so water couldn't enter or escape until one of the trapdoors was opened. When the top one was opened, the holding tank would fill with water from the exhibit so the diver could swim in with the turtle and then close the door, locking them safely inside, sealed off from the four hundred thousand gallons of water above. Opening the bottom trapdoor would then release the water contained in the holding tank, allowing the diver to lower the turtle with the hydraulic lift (so they wouldn't go plummeting to the floor like I had) and presumably escape with the stolen reptilian booty. If they had some kind of cart or mobile turtle tank, they could then pull it, and the five-hundred-pound giant turtle, along the old tracks to freedom.

So where was that five-hundred-pound turtle now?

The tunnel looked like it had been there forever, but if I was right about the trapdoor and the hydraulic lift, somebody had very recently put a lot of thought and effort into transforming it into an escape route. Frank totally would have geeked out over the design of it all. I just needed to find a way out so I could tell him about it.

I shone the light down the tunnel, which just disappeared into more darkness. I looked back up at the trapdoor. Even if I wanted to go back through the holding tank, there was still a giant angry shark up there waiting for me. Plus, I'd lost my regulator and Octo backup—and there was no way I was going to chance a free swim through shark-infested water without a breathing apparatus.

"Okay, Joe," I said to myself (the silence was really starting to get to me), "I guess we're hoofing it." I stuffed my heavy dive gear, including my flippers, over to the side of the tunnel, though I was still wearing my wet suit and dive boots.

The tunnel went on for a few hundred yards before it started to branch off into a network of smaller tunnels to who knows where. Some of them were already caved in under a pile of rubble. I was sticking to the main tunnel.

My right foot slid out from under me, and I caught myself before I could fall. When I shone my light down at the ground to see what I had slipped on, it reflected off something white. There was a muddy piece of fabric lying in the dirt. It didn't look like much, but there was something about this particular dirty white cloth that told me it could be an important clue.

My flashlight started to flicker. Not good. It must have been damaged in the fall. If it died and I was left down there in the dark, that tunnel was going to turn into my tomb. Time to get moving. I stuffed the cloth in my dive belt to examine more closely once I made it back to daylight. If I made it back to daylight.

After a few minutes I reached an intersection, branching left and right. I shone my light left—another endless tunnel into darkness—and right, where it looked like there might be, just maybe, a glimmer of daylight at the end of the tunnel. Right it was.

Right turned out to be the right call. A few minutes later,

I climbed a rickety ladder and found myself in the boiler room of an abandoned warehouse. I looked around for any sign that Captain Hook had been there. There was nothing. The thief must have smuggled the turtle out of one of the other tunnels.

I made my way out onto the dock and took a deep breath, grateful to be out of the musty tunnel and back aboveground in the fresh air. Unfortunately, the air aboveground wasn't much better. A potpourri of fish guts and diesel fumes greeted me. I looked around and realized the aromas must have been coming from the old cannery a few lots down and a passing container ship.

That's when I spotted Frank on the water taxi.

I don't know who was more shocked when we saw each other, Frank or me. I must have looked pretty funny, jumping up and down on the dock in my wet suit, waving my arms like a crazy person. Man, was it good to see him again. After the run-in with the shark and stumbling around in the tunnels, I hadn't been sure I'd get another chance.

Once Frank had disembarked from the boat, I brought him up to date on everything that had happened since Bruce had so rudely interrupted our underwater investigation of Predator Reef. Then he filled me in on his chase with the hooded perp.

"Um, I didn't want to tell you this," Frank said when he finished. "But Aly kind of makes sense as a possible suspect."

"No way, dude," I said. "Aly wouldn't have—"

But then I stopped and thought about it for a second.

"She did conveniently disappear right before someone released Bruce, and I guess she would have had access to the shark tank."

"And earlier today she was wearing the same kind of baggy aquarium hoodie as the perp I chased," Frank said. "I didn't get close enough to tell if it was a guy or a girl, but we can't rule out the possibility it was her."

"Ugh," I said, closing my eyes. Could the girl I liked actually want me dead? Why does this have to happen every time? Whenever I like a girl, one of our cases never fails to gum things up.

"Any other ideas who it could have been?" I asked, hoping he'd give me the name of someone I wasn't interested in dating. "Or how Aly might tie in with the tunnel under the aquarium?"

"No idea, but I bet the tunnel you found is from the Underground Railroad like the one the history museum is giving tours of across town," he said excitedly. "They've only excavated a few hundred feet of that one, but they think there may have once been a whole network of them. Imagine, a hundred and fifty years ago, escaped slaves could have made their way to freedom through the same tunnel you were in."

Yep, trust my bro to give a history lecture at a time like this.

"If the one across town is a part of the same network of tunnels as the ones I found, then the thief could have taken Captain Hook anywhere in Bayport," I said.

"Okay, so we've solved part of the mystery. We know

how she was taken, but we still don't know who did it or where they took her." Frank was stumped. I could see the wheels turning inside his brain. "It doesn't really help us, but there are rumors that pirates originally built the tunnels as far back as the 1600s to smuggle their plunder in and out of the port," he said, the nerd in him unable to resist adding another chapter to the history lesson.

"I guess that would explain why there are old tracks in the tunnels, but I don't think it was pirates who took Captain Hook, even if she is named after one." I couldn't help but laugh at the image of a bunch of pirate turtles abducting their pirate turtle captain.

"Well, at least now we know that whoever did take her must have had access to the exhibit when it was being constructed. There wouldn't have been any way to build that escape hatch after the exhibit was filled with water," Frank said, narrowing down the suspect list.

I narrowed it down further.

"That's not all, though," I told Frank as I pulled out the muddy piece of cloth. I'd gotten a chance to look at it a little more closely while I'd been waiting for Frank and the water taxi to reach the dock. "I found this trampled down in the dirt. I wouldn't even have seen it if I hadn't almost slipped on it."

"What is it?" Frank asked. "A handkerchief?"

"Not just a handkerchief," I said, brushing it off to reveal the monogrammed initials B.V. "Mr. V's handkerchief."

10 THE SECRET LAIR

FRANK

WE BOTH FIGURED A SURPRISE visit to Mr. V was in order. A half hour later we had changed into street clothes and hopped back aboard a water taxi headed to his mansion. When he moved to Bayport to start construction on Predator Reef, he'd bought himself a big old house right across the bay on a hill overlooking the harbor so he could see the aquarium from his back porch.

"There are only so many ways one of Mr. V's handkerchiefs could have made its way into a four-hundred-year-old tunnel," my brother said, shielding his eyes from the sun.

"Yeah. And the most obvious one was that he dropped it there a lot more recently than four hundred years ago," I replied.

Just then my phone buzzed with a text from Big Chuck.

"I've got news about the shark that attacked you," I told Joe after reading it. "Big Chuck says that once they finally got Bruce back in the examination tank, they discovered the reason he went all *Jaws* on us."

"Because private detectives taste good?" Joe cracked.

"No, because someone jabbed him in the side with enough force to break through the shark's tough skin," I said. "Someone wanted him angry. He's usually a really calm shark; he never would have gone after you like that unless he was pretty incensed."

"You think Mr. V had something to do with that, too?"

I was quiet for a second. I didn't like the idea that Mr. V might be capable of harming an animal.

"I guess we'll see."

When we got to Mr. V's and walked around to the front of the property, we could see news vans camped out in front of his house. I guess they didn't think we were newsworthy, because they let us walk right past. I pressed the buzzer on the mansion's big double doors. After a few minutes, the tuxedoed chauffeur who resembled Alfred from *Batman* opened the door. Like Alfred, I guess he was the butler as well as the chauffeur. He looked at us like we were a couple of unwelcome salesmen.

"Yes, how may I help you?" he said in the same strong New England accent as Mr. V and Ron. From the way they sounded, Mr. V must have recruited everyone on his staff from the same place.

"We're here to see Mr. Valledor," I said.

"I'm sure you are," Alfred said. It was hard to tell if he was peering down his nose at us or if it was just the way his face looked. "Mr. Valledor is a very busy man. I don't suppose you have an appointment?"

"No, but I think he'll want to hear what we have to say," Joe told him.

"We'll see." Alfred sounded unconvinced. "And who might Mr. Valledor have the, ahem, pleasure of meeting unannounced?"

"You can tell him it's the Hardy boys," I said. "He knows who we are."

He replied by slamming the big door in our faces. He opened it again a couple of minutes later.

"Follow me," he said.

We walked through the mansion's grand entrance hall into a large study, where Mr. V was seated with Ron Burris and Laura, the assistant we had met earlier.

"The young men you wished to see, sir," Alfred announced.

"Thank you, Jonathan," he said to Alfred, whose name turned out not to be Alfred at all.

Mr. V motioned for us to come in. "This is a welcome surprise. When I heard the doorbell, I assumed it was another reporter hounding me for an interview about Captain Hook."

"Sir," Alfred (aka Jonathan) interrupted, seeming rather put out by the whole affair. "Will there be anything else?"

"Yes, Jonathan," he said. "We were just wrapping up here. If you could see Ron and Laura out?"

This seemed to be news to Ron.

"But Bradley, we still haven't figured out what we're going to do about the delays at the underwater hotel site in Helsinki," Ron protested.

"I trust you to handle it," Mr. V said. "Right now I'd like to speak to Frank and Joe."

Ron had been nice before, but now he looked at us like we were a couple of mosquitoes intent on annoying him.

"Bradley, there's a lot of money at stake here. I really think we need to focus on what's important. I know you're concerned about the turtle—we all are—but—" Ron didn't get to finish the sentence.

"But I pay you a very good salary to handle my company's public relations," Mr. V snapped. "What I choose to do with my private time is my business."

"Yes, sir, I understand," Ron mumbled. He closed his briefcase and walked out of the study, hanging his head like a kid who'd been sent to his room without dinner.

"Are you sure you don't want me to stay, Mr. V?" Laura asked, sounding more like an overprotective parent than a young assistant.

"Thank you, Laura, but I think the Hardy boys and I should be just fine on our own," he replied.

"I'll be on standby if you need me," she said, forcing a smile as she followed Ron out the door.

"Sir?" Jonathan asked.

"You too, Jonathan, thank you," he said. "I'll call you if we need anything."

Jonathan gave us another nasty look before leaving us alone with Mr. V.

"My apologies for my staff's lack of hospitality. Running a company can be a bit like being the head of a household, and like many large families, I'm afraid my team and I tend to be a bit dysfunctional at times. And with the news cameras pounding down the door about Captain Hook, we're all a bit on edge," Mr. V. said. "So, have you made any progress?"

Joe didn't answer. Instead he pulled out the dirty handkerchief with Mr. V's initials on it.

"I'm sorry, but I don't understand," Mr. V said as he stared at the handkerchief. "Is that mine?"

"Want to guess where we found it?" Joe asked.

"I don't have any idea, why—"

"I'll give you a hint. It was somewhere it shouldn't have been," Joe said.

"In a tunnel under four hundred thousand gallons of water," I added. "Maybe you can tell us how it got there?"

"I—" Mr. V started, then closed his mouth. A moment later, he gave us a weak smile. "You are even better detectives than I had been led to believe."

He stood up. "I have a confession to make."

Now it was our turn to be speechless. Was Mr. V about to admit to stealing Captain Hook?

"If you'll follow me, there is something I'd like to show you." Mr. V turned and began walking down the hall at the far end of the room.

My brother and I exchanged a grim look. Normally, we'd be a lot more cautious before blindly following a suspect somewhere, but curiosity had the better of us. We let him lead us down a spiral staircase and past a long corridor to a library at the back of the house.

It was an ocean lover's dream. The shelves were lined with endless leather-bound volumes and academic texts with titles like *The Early Voyages of Jacques Cousteau*, *Biodiversity in the Indo-Pacific Reef Environment*, and *Advances in Submersible Design and Technology*. I could have spent a month flipping through the pages and been totally happy! The room was decorated with all kinds of nautical artifacts and maps. There were saltwater fish tanks too, some filled with specimens so rare even Bayport Aquarium didn't have them.

But all that was nothing compared to what we were about to see.

Mr. V ran his fingers along a row of books, settling on one with a battered leather spine and pulling it toward him.

Joe and I stood there with our mouths hanging open as the entire wall slid away, revealing a secret lair that rivaled the Batcave in coolness.

We were staring at Mr. V's own magnificent private aquarium.

The twelve-foot-high walls were made entirely of floor-to-ceiling glass. Behind them must have been at least two hundred thousand gallons of salt water filled with a flowing kelp forest and an array of awesome creatures, including rays and small sharks. It may not have been as big as Predator Reef, but to find something like this hidden inside a house made it just as impressive. It felt like we were standing underwater in the middle of a vast seascape.

"This was to be Captain Hook's new home," Mr. V said quietly.

Joe and I shared a glance, reading each other's minds. There was no doubt anymore that Bradley Valledor was the one who'd built the escape hatch beneath Predator Reef.

"I'm ashamed to admit that there were selfish motivations for my participation in the aquarium's new exhibit," he said. "Still, I pride myself on being a conservationist as well as a collector. When Captain Hook arrived at the Bayport Aquarium, I saw the perfect chance to acquire a rare and remarkable creature for my collection without supporting the poaching trade or taking one of the precious few remaining animals from the wild."

"So you pretended to be helping the aquarium by building Predator Reef when the whole time you intended to steal its mascot and betray the entire community?!" I asked in disbelief.

"I probably deserve your disgust, but let me finish and then you can render judgment," Mr. V said. "I discovered the tunnels beneath the aquarium during my initial planning and designed the hidden holding tank under the exhibit to take advantage of them." He took a deep breath. "So yes, I confess . . ."

Here it came, the big confession. Villains don't normally lure detectives to their secret lairs just to reveal their master plans, though. Not unless they also intend on disposing of said detectives so they can't tattle to the authorities. So by this point, I was beginning to expect the worst.

". . . I was the architect of the crime," he continued in a shaky voice. "But I wasn't the one who committed it. Someone else took Captain Hook before I had the chance."

I was too baffled to respond. Had Mr. V just confessed to the crime or hadn't he?

"I thought I could provide a good home for her, one that was even better than the aquarium. One that would leave her in peace without being gawked at by thousands of observers each day." Mr. V paused.

"Gawked at?!" I couldn't believe what he was saying. "You're supposed to be a conservationist! I thought you understood better than anyone how much the aquarium inspires a love of the ocean and educates people about ecology."

"I know." Mr. V turned away, unable to look me in the eye. "And as it turns out, my first impression was wrong.

I saw how much Captain Hook thrived in Predator Reef, how much the staff cared for her, the difference she could make in the fight for oceanic conservation. And I started to second-guess myself. Apparently whoever discovered my plans didn't share my reservations."

"C'mon, dude. You really expect us to believe your sob story?" Joe said.

"I know it won't be easy to regain your trust, but why would I bring you here to my private sanctuary and reveal my plans to you, only to lie about this?" Mr. V asked in response.

"You've already admitted to lying about everything else," I challenged. "How do we know you aren't just hiding her in a different location and trying to throw us off your trail?"

"Had I wanted to deflect suspicion, I simply would have kept my mouth shut and called my lawyers. A discarded handkerchief is explained away easily enough. And I certainly wouldn't have insisted to Chief Olaf on your participation in the investigation."

Mr. V was making sense, but . . .

"If you really cared so much about finding Captain Hook, why didn't you come forward earlier? We lost valuable time on the investigation, and my brother almost got killed finding that trapdoor."

"Until you boys arrived this afternoon with my handkerchief and your tales of hidden tunnels, I'd held out hope that you or the police would uncover another explanation for Captain Hook's disappearance or discover the tunnels in a way that didn't incriminate me. It was selfish of me."

"You bet it was," Joe said.

"Frank knows as well as anyone how much that turtle means to me. I dote on her like a spoiled child. I've spent so much time with her, it almost feels like she really is family. Now that she's gone . . ." Mr. V closed his eyes. "The thought that I may have accidentally helped someone with bad . . . intentions," he murmured brokenly, "take her . . . it's been torturing me. Which is why I've decided to bring you here and confess my role."

"Sure, you feel guilty. You want to clear your conscience to make yourself feel better. So do lots of criminals. That doesn't change the fact that Captain Hook is missing and it's your fault," I told him.

Mr. V turned around again to face us.

"It's not my conscience I'm concerned with. It's the life of an innocent animal. I want you to help me get her back. I know now that her rightful home isn't here," he said, gesturing at the marvelous tank behind him. "It's at the aquarium where everyone can enjoy her company and learn from her. I hope it doesn't come to this, but I am willing to turn myself in and face the consequences as long as it means Captain Hook is safely returned to the aquarium."

Mr. V stopped and looked both of us in the eye.

"Even if it means going to prison."

11 CRUSHED

JOE

I DIDN'T KNOW WHAT TO THINK ABOUT MR. V or his confession. Somehow we'd managed to solve what we'd thought was the mystery without solving the crime. We now knew how Captain Hook was taken and we even knew who'd planned to take her, but we still didn't know who actually had taken her.

As mad as I was at Mr. V, I believed that he hadn't taken her and that he was heartbroken about the fact that some-one had.

But if Bradley Valledor didn't do it, Frank and I had to find out who did. And we had to find out fast. Captain Hook's life was in danger. Every hour that went by might turn out to be an hour too late.

Since Mr. V had created this mess, I was hoping he could help us clean it up.

"So if we're to believe you, you're a criminal mastermind without actually being the criminal," I said once we were back in his study.

"I . . ." Mr. V hesitated. "I wouldn't put it that way, but I suppose so, yes."

"Well, if you're not the bad guy, then who is?" Frank asked the million-dollar question.

"I don't know how anyone would have found out about the hidden tank. My firm's own architects didn't even know, and neither did anyone on the construction crew. I made sure of it."

"I saw that escape hatch," I said. "It's not like you threw that thing together at the last minute with a handful of Legos. It's a complicated piece of engineering. How do you build something like that into the exhibit without anyone on the construction crew knowing about it?"

Mr. V smiled self-consciously. Things had gone terribly wrong, but you could tell he was still proud of his plan.

"It wasn't easy, but by designing and overseeing the construction of the exhibit myself, I was able to divide up the labor so different workers handled only small parts of the secret holding tank without knowing what those parts were for . . . or what anyone else was doing, for that matter. That way no one would suspect anything out of the ordinary."

"Yeah, but it didn't work out that way, did it, dude?" I said.

Mr. V looked down at his feet. "But I was so careful. I don't know what went wrong."

"What about the rest of your staff? Laura and Ron and the others?" Frank asked.

"No one knew who wasn't supposed to," Mr. V said. "Not my family, not Ron, not anyone else."

"I noticed you didn't mention Laura's name," I pointed out.

"Or Jonathan's," Frank added.

"So there were going to be other people in on the heist with you?" I asked, reading between the lines. "Couldn't they have gone through with it behind your back?"

"Absolutely not," Mr. V insisted. "I trust my inner circle completely. They wouldn't betray me."

"People will do a lot of things you don't think they would if there's enough money at stake," I told him.

"Not my people," he said.

"We're still going to need to talk to them," Frank said. "Even if they weren't involved, they may have information that helps us."

Jonathan appeared at the door before Mr. V had a chance to respond.

"You have another unscheduled visitor, sir," Jonathan announced.

Mr. V's face burst into a huge smile when he saw the

young lady who walked in the door behind Jonathan. Mine, on the other hand, fell.

"Boys, have you met my niece Aly?"

Frank threw me a quick glance. Sometimes I wish we weren't able to read each other so well. I knew he was thinking the thing about Aly that I was trying not to. Even if Mr. V was in denial about it, it was possible that someone close to him could have secretly gained access to his plans—making his favorite niece, and my favorite scuba instructor, even more of a suspect.

Being an expert diver and a member of the BAD team, Aly had free, unsupervised access to Predator Reef. That gave her both the means and the opportunity to have committed the crime.

Supercute Aly hadn't just walked in the door of Mr. V's study. She'd also moved straight to the top of our suspects list.

"Joe?" she said, sounding just as surprised to see me. "What are you doing here?"

"Hey Aly, we were, uh . . ." I fumbled for the right thing to say. I had a feeling this could get real awkward real quick. Mr. V stepped in to save me.

"The Hardy boys and I were just discussing the investigation into Captain Hook's disappearance," Mr. V said.

Aly gave me a look I couldn't quite read. To the paranoid detective in me, it seemed like a hostile one. It also occurred to me that if she'd had something to do with releasing the shark into Predator Reef, she might be surprised to see me alive.

I'd have to save that particular disturbing thought for later, though. Jonathan had just walked back into the room carrying a phone.

"Call for you, sir," he said to Mr. V.

"Take a message if you could, Jonathan. I'm in the midst of some pressing matters."

"They say it's urgent, sir," Jonathan said, holding out the phone to his employer.

Mr. V looked annoyed. "Who is it?"

"They wouldn't say, sir. They said they'd only speak to you." He lowered his voice. "It's about the turtle."

Mr. V took the phone and lifted it to his ear.

"Yes," he demanded. A moment later his expression turned to one of horror. He lowered the phone.

"They say to have the reward money ready in one hour or we'll never see Captain Hook alive again."

PROOF OF LIFE

12

FRANK

THIS WAS IT. THE RANSOM CALL.

All this time, we had wondered about the motivation for the crime. As is so often the case, the crook was after money. It gave us hope that Captain Hook wasn't bound for some witch doctor's pot. At least not yet.

As an international businessman, Mr. V seemed to know his way around a negotiation. The first thing he did when he got back on the phone was to demand "proof of life"; that's what it's called when the kidnapper provides some kind of proof that the victim is still alive before a ransom is paid.

The kidnapper hung up, and a minute later Mr. V received a photo text on his cell phone. It was dark and out of focus, but there was no question it was Captain Hook.

She was partially submerged in a tiny tank that looked like a hot tub on wheels. It was heartbreaking to see her like that.

Mr. V turned to his niece. "I'm sorry, darling, but we'll have to catch up later. Right now I need to speak to Frank and Joe alone."

Aly had something else in mind.

"No way, Uncle Brad. I have as much right to know what's going on with Captain Hook as they do."

"I'm sorry, I can't let you get mixed up in the middle of a kidnapping investigation," Mr. V said. "It's too dangerous."

"Dangerous?!" she said, laughing him off. "You need to have a better reason than that, Uncle Brad. In case you forgot, I'm a master diver. I think I can handle dangerous."

"I didn't mean to insinuate that you can't, darling, it's just—" Mr. V started, but Aly wasn't having any of it.

"Just what? That you trust them to help more than your own niece?" Aly waved her hand dismissively in our direction. Getting shut out by her uncle just as there was a break in the case had her pretty heated.

"Aly, dear, it's not—" Mr. V tried to protest, but Aly cut him off again.

"I'm just as qualified to deal with danger as they are. I go swimming with sharks every day." She shot Joe a look before adding, "And I've never almost been eaten by one."

It looked like Mr. V picking us to stay over Aly had turned Joe into the competition. I could tell he felt burned. It didn't help that Aly could have been the one to plan the episode that almost turned my brother into shark food. Joe didn't say anything, though. This argument was between Aly and Mr. V. Tempers were hot, and we were just caught in the crossfire.

"I've spent more time with Captain Hook than either of them. And I'm family. They're not," Aly added, emphasizing the point.

"Which is exactly why I want to keep you safe," Mr. V tried to explain.

"This is totally unfair," she complained. "You're really going to choose a couple of strangers over me? You don't need to protect me. You should just tell me what you know about the kidnapping and let me decide for myself if I can help."

"The truth is that there are things I need to discuss with the boys that could get us all in a lot of trouble with the police, and I can't let you be involved."

That caused Joe and me to exchange a look. What else hadn't Mr. V told us?

I think Aly could tell her uncle wasn't going to give in, but she didn't look happy about it.

"Fine," Aly conceded. "But promise me you'll call me as soon as you hear anything. If you don't . . ."

"You'd probably kick my butt. I know, my dear," Mr. V said with a sad smile. "You have my word."

He gave his niece a hug before she left.

"Bye, Aly," Joe said tentatively.

Aly walked out the door without looking in his direction.

I felt bad for my brother. I knew he liked Aly a lot, and I didn't think her appearance in the middle of our case was going to do much to help his romantic prospects. Something was bothering me more than Joe's love life, though.

"What did you mean about us getting in trouble with the police?" I demanded. We weren't strangers to Chief Olaf's bad side, but we certainly weren't looking for new reasons to get into his doghouse. Or worse, a jail cell. He'd threatened it enough times, and I didn't think he'd hesitate to make good on his threat if we gave him a good enough reason.

"The kidnapper said if he sees any sign of the police, he'll kill Captain Hook," Mr. V replied.

"It sounds like a bluff to me," Joe said. "Not with that much money on the line."

"I'm not willing to take that chance," Mr. V said. "That's why I want you boys to handle the drop."

I wasn't expecting that. But Mr. V was right. Chief Olaf most definitely would not approve of Joe and me going behind his back and confronting a kidnapper on our own.

"I know it's risky. Frankly, it's more than I have a right to ask, so I won't think any less of you if you decline," Mr. V said.

"Count us in," I said. I didn't even have to look at Joe to know he was with me.

Mr. V gave a solemn nod. "It's settled then. I would go myself, but the press has been following me, angling for a scoop, ever since I left the aquarium this morning. Jonathan," he said to his butler, "please go to the safe and pack two briefcases for Frank and Joe."

The kidnapper called again a minute later. We were to take the money to a construction site a few blocks from the harbor and await further instructions. Mr. V had his own plan, which the kidnapper had agreed to: insisting that the payment be made in two parts—half up front and half after Captain Hook was safely back in our possession. It was quick thinking on Mr. V's part. That way the kidnapper had incentive to make good on his promise to deliver the turtle and, more importantly, not to harm us after we handed him the first installment.

"Do any of the tunnels have an entrance near there?" I asked Mr. V, hoping he might be able to provide us with some intel about Captain Hook's potential location.

"I don't know," he said. "I designed my plan around use of the main tunnel, since that was the most direct route. I didn't have time to map the others."

A short time later, Joe and I were in the back of Mr. V's Rolls-Royce with half a million in cash each. Jonathan let Joe out in front of the construction site with the first briefcase, while I snuck around the corner with briefcase number two to provide backup if needed.

Joe stood in the construction site's empty parking lot and waited. After a few minutes, someone called out from the shadows. Whoever it was, they were trying to disguise their voice, but it sounded familiar—and it was definitely a man's. I couldn't quite place it, though.

"Do you have the money?" the kidnapper asked.

"Half of it," Joe called back. "You get the second half after I get the turtle."

"Leave the briefcase in the middle of the lot and then walk back to the street and I'll bring out the turtle," the voice said.

"I need to see the turtle first." Joe played it cool.

"No. The money first, then the turtle."

"Not gonna happen," Joe said.

"Do it now or the turtle is toast!" the kidnapper yelled.

"Not until you show me Captain Hook," Joe said, calling the turtle-napper's bluff. "If you even have her."

The turtle-napper was getting flustered. This apparently wasn't going the way he had planned. "I'm not messing around! The turtle gets it if you don't give me the briefcase!"

"You don't have her, do you?" Joe said.

"I do so! Now give me the money!"

"No can do." Joe kept his cool.

The perp didn't. "I have a gun! Now put down the briefcase!"

If Joe was afraid, he didn't show it.

The turtle-napper stepped out of the shadows, and I gasped. It was the same hooded figure I'd chased across the harbor earlier that day. His face was still hidden by the hoodie and sunglasses, and his hand was jammed in the sweatshirt's pocket holding something that could have been a gun. As a general rule, if someone really has a gun, they'll show it to you, but there was no way to tell for sure if this guy was bluffing until he did or didn't pull the trigger. There are some mistakes you never got a chance to learn from.

"Drop the briefcase or I'll shoot!" he yelled again, stepping closer.

"Hey, I know that voice!" Joe said.

That's when the perp panicked. He pulled his hand from his pocket. It wasn't a gun at all. It was a chunk of brick. And he hurled it right at Joe's head. When Joe lifted his briefcase to deflect the brick, the perp charged. The brick ricocheted off the case and glanced off Joe's knuckles.

"Argh!" he cried.

I sprinted from my hiding place, trying to intersect Joe's assailant. The assailant got there first and slammed into Joe. He was able to tear the briefcase out of Joe's wounded hand, but he didn't make it far. The second he got up to make a run for it, I leveled him with a clean tackle. He didn't even see me coming.

As he lay on the ground, trying to catch his wind, I yanked back his hood to reveal . . .

"Carter?"

13 STILL MISSING

JOE

"FIGURES," I SAID.

Even with my knuckles throbbing from their encounter with the brick, I still couldn't help laughing. No wonder the kidnapper had botched the ransom attempt. Carter was, to put it nicely, a bozo. Seriously, what had Aly ever seen in this guy?

I looked at the bloody gash where the chunk of brick had clocked me and checked the sudden impulse to hit him. It's okay to defend yourself if you have to, but I wasn't about to sink to Carter's level and sucker punch an unarmed person. I helped my brother hold him down instead.

"Let me go!" he yelled.

"The only place you're going to is jail. Now where's the

turtle?" I demanded. Frank and I held Carter down tightly. He wasn't getting away.

"I don't have her, I swear. I just made it up so I could get the money."

"This is the last time. Where is Captain Hook?" My patience was running out.

"I swear, I don't know. I didn't do anything wrong!"

Didn't do anything wrong? Carter was even more clueless than I thought.

"You don't call extortion and assault and battery doing anything wrong?"

"And why did you run from me at the aquarium? Or were you just going for an afternoon jog?" Frank asked.

"It wasn't my fault! I didn't want to have anything to do with it. Someone made me."

Now we were getting somewhere.

"Who? Who made you?"

"I don't know who it was. I never saw them. I don't know where the turtle is. I don't know anything. Please, I swear." Carter had started to ramble.

"That doesn't make any sense, Carter. You obviously saw the turtle. We saw the picture you sent Mr. Valledor." Frank tried using logic. I could have told him he was wasting his time.

"I saw the turtle, but not who took her. They blindfolded me."

"So you're telling us you were just minding your own

business and the thief randomly decided it would be fun to blindfold you and show you the turtle against your will?" I asked, laughing at the ridiculousness of it. "Why risk exposing themselves to you of all people? I know it wasn't because of your brains."

"They found out I was stealing fish from the aquarium, okay? They threatened to turn me in if I didn't help."

That meshed with what Murph had picked up about someone stealing rare fish and selling them to collectors online. Carter's list of felonies just kept on getting longer.

"Help do what?" Frank asked.

"Steal Captain Hook's medicine, since I had access to the lab. I guess they didn't know she needed special medication until they saw Mr. V's press conference," Carter said. The BAD team worked closely with the vets who were treating her, so that part made sense at least.

"Whoever it was blindfolded me and took me to some warehouse or someplace, I don't know where. I showed them how to inject the turtle's meds, and then they dropped me off. The person was wearing a mask, so I didn't see a face. I was able to snap the picture without them seeing before they put the blindfold back on, but that's all I saw."

At least he'd done something right.

"Why did you sic the shark on us?" I wanted to know. "That's why you ran away from Frank when Bruce attacked me, isn't it?"

"I didn't mean to," Carter said meekly.

"Um, how do you accidentally release a four-hundred-pound predatory fish?" Frank asked.

Yeah, I was kind of wondering about that myself.

"Bruce was in the holding tank, waiting for a routine checkup. I figured you were onto me when you started snooping around, and I thought if I released the shark, it would scare you off. I didn't mean for him to attack you."

"What about the puncture mark in Bruce's side? Was that an accident too?" Frank accused.

For what it's worth, Carter actually looked like he felt bad about that one. "Oh, I didn't mean to hurt him. I guess I poked him harder than I thought. It's the only way I could get him to leave the holding tank."

Just our luck that it got him so riled up that he tried to eat me. Carter wasn't winning himself any points with the Hardy boys, that was for sure. And his appearance only made the mystery more, well, mysterious.

This was the second time in a matter of hours we'd thought we'd solved the crime only to discover it was more complicated than we could have imagined. We'd found out who devised the original plan (Mr. V) and who tried to kill us (Carter), but we still didn't know who stole Captain Hook. I was really starting to get frustrated. Were our mystery-solving skills getting rusty?

"It's about time you tell us something that actually helps us, or this is going to get really ugly for you, dude," I warned. "Unless you want to spend the rest of your life in prison."

Frank picked up on my bad-cop tactic and assumed the role of good cop.

"You're in a lot of trouble, Carter," he said calmly. "If you can help us find Captain Hook before she gets hurt, then it will really help your case, especially if we put in a good word for you with the chief."

"I don't know anything else. I'd tell you if I did," he pleaded.

It was my turn.

"What do you think Aly's gonna think when she finds out you helped the guy who kidnapped Captain Hook? You think she'll take you back then, huh, babe?" I said, adding just a touch of extra force with my knee as I held him down. Carter groaned. I kind of liked playing the bad cop.

"Think, Carter. There has to be something," Frank coaxed. "What did the person's voice sound like?"

"I don't know." Carter whimpered. The guy was close to turning into a blubbering mess.

"Sheesh, Carter, how do you not know what they sounded like?" I asked. "Did they communicate with you telepathically?"

"It sounded weird, like they did something to change their voice. It was all robotic."

Another dead end. Whoever it was had obviously been a lot smarter than Carter.

"If they used an electronic voice distorter, it could be really hard to identify them," I said to Frank.

"Yeah, but not impossible," Frank replied. "Most distorters aren't perfect. You can sometimes still pick up clues from a person's speech patterns."

"Was there anything they said that might give them away?" I asked Carter.

"Was it a guy? A girl?" Frank asked, forcing me to think about the fact that Aly was still out there as a suspect.

"I—I don't know," he stuttered. At this point, Carter had given up struggling altogether and was just lying there like a useless bump on a log.

I sighed. "Let's just tell the chief he wouldn't cooperate and be done with it."

"Wait," Carter said. "There was something maybe. Some of the things they said sounded kind of funny."

"Of course they sounded funny, dude, they were using a voice distorter," I groaned in exasperation.

"No, like a different kind of funny. Like they said some of the words in a funny way," Carter tried to explain. "Like maybe they were from a different country, you know, like they were British or something."

Frank and I looked at each other. There was only one person we knew in Bayport who fit that description.

Dirk Bishop.

14
SOMETHING FISHY

FRANK

NOW WE HAD A SOLID LEAD. THE ARROgant black market treasure hunter from jolly old England was skilled, savvy, and shady enough to have pulled it off. And there wasn't anyone in Bayport who better knew how to move hot goods. This wasn't just gold coins, though. Gold coins don't have a pulse and they don't feel pain. The "rare goods" we were looking for had a lot more value than a price tag. If Bishop planned to move Captain Hook, we had to find out where and when before it was too late.

And those ends were still dead. Carter hadn't been able to give us a single usable clue about where Captain Hook had been taken. Even if we wanted to risk exploring the network of tunnels Joe had found, it could take days to figure out where every corridor went—and that's if one of the tunnels didn't collapse on us. We wouldn't do Captain Hook much good buried under a pile of rubble.

"Think, Carter. Is there anything else you remember about where this person took you? Anything at all?" I asked.

"I think it was like an old warehouse or something," he said.

That was about as useful as him telling us it was somewhere in Bayport. The port was lined with old warehouses. Even with a huge search party, checking them all could take forever.

"Can you remember anything about where the car you were in may have gone? Like going over railroad tracks or hearing factory sounds?"

"No, nothing like that. I mean it smelled really fishy, you know, but that's all."

I'm not sure how much of a lead that was—the bay was full of fish—but something about it caught Joe's interest.

"Like normal wharf fishy or extra-stinky fishy?" Joe asked.

"Like really stinky fishy," Carter said, actually sounding confident about something for once.

Joe nodded. "It's a long shot, but I think I have an idea where it could have been."

"I'm listening," I said.

"When I came out of the tunnel in that warehouse, it wasn't far from the old cannery. I could smell the fish guts all the way from there, even though it was a few lots farther down the port."

It made sense. I'd seen something in the news a few months back about the cannery going out of business. They shut it down, but I guess they couldn't get rid of the smell. It was abandoned, it was near enough to the tunnel Joe had found, and it stank of fish.

"It's worth a look," I said.

"It's the only lead we've got," Joe agreed.

"Sirs," someone said from behind us, and we both jumped.

When we looked up, Jonathan was standing over us holding a length of rope, looking particularly sinister. He was pretty sneaky for an old guy in a tuxedo. He'd walked right up behind us without us even noticing. I wasn't sure how long he'd been eavesdropping.

"For the prisoner, sirs," he said, holding up the rope.

I didn't know if Jonathan was keeping an eye on us at Mr. V's request or if he had his own agenda. I wasn't sure if we could trust him, but he and his Rolls were the quickest way for us to get where we wanted to go.

"Jonathan, can you drive us to the closest water taxi stop?" I asked, hedging our bets. If he could drop us at the water taxi stop on this side of the port, we could save some time by taking it across to the cannery and wouldn't have to reveal to Jonathan where we were going (if he hadn't overheard already).

"If I must," he replied as we tied up Carter.

Once we got there, we left Carter and the briefcases full of cash with Jonathan and hopped a water taxi. The stink from the cannery got stronger the closer we got. We had the water taxi let us off by the warehouse next door so we could sneak up on the cannery without being seen.

I had second thoughts as soon as we slipped inside the cannery through a cracked back door. The abandoned industrial building with its hanging hooks, conveyor belts, and strange mechanical devices was downright spooky, especially with all the eerie shadows everywhere. "Do those look like footprints?" Joe asked in a hushed voice.

He was pointing to a shadowy corner where a trail of dirt spilled out from under a closed utility closet door. When we got over to the closet, Joe leaned down and rubbed some of the dirt between his fingers.

He gave me a serious look.

"Same dirt as in the tunnel."

Which meant we were going to have to open that door. Anytime you open a closed door in a hostile environment, you have to be prepared for the possibility that someone, or something, will jump out at you. Joe and I had done this more than a few times, and we weren't about to be caught by surprise.

Using hand signals so we couldn't be overheard, we quickly coordinated our plan of attack—Joe to the left of the door, me to the right, both of us ready to either storm in or pounce on whatever leaped out.

I reached for the knob, ready to throw the door open, not sure what we were going to find on the other side. The door opened with a creak and then silence. There was no one inside, man or turtle.

There was more dirt on the floor, though, and oddly, it seemed to disappear under the closet's back wall. At this point in our investigation, I had a pretty good idea what to expect next.

"Trapdoor," Joe said.

Sure enough, we were able to pop out a panel in the wall. Behind it was the entrance to the tunnel.

"Well, we found his entry point, but still no sign of Captain Hook," I said. "Let's scan the closet for clues."

I wasn't sure if what we found next was good news or bad news.

The discarded red scuba tank hidden behind a bucket of mops must have been what the thief used to swim up into Predator Reef to nab Captain Hook. That meant we were definitely in the right place.

The discarded veterinary syringe with blood on its tip was a lot more frightening.

"She was here, Joe."

"Her and Carter both," Joe agreed. "If this is where the kidnapper brought Carter, that means Captain Hook was here just a few hours ago."

But she wasn't there now. Joe and I stared at the syringe. It was an all too gruesome reminder of just how much danger she was in. I had the awful feeling that we were too late. That Captain Hook was already gone.

"Where to now?" Joe asked. I shook my head. I didn't know.

"The street-side entrance to the cannery is blocked off, so if he was going to move her to another location, it probably would have been from the waterfront and not the road," I reasoned.

We made our way cautiously to the berths where fishing boats used to dock to unload their catch. A narrow wooden pier led between the cannery and an abandoned shipyard, where the canned fish had once been loaded onto container ships.

Which meant the small container ship we saw with Chinese characters painted on its side had no business preparing to dock alongside it.

"That shouldn't be there, should it?" Joe asked.

"Not unless they're picking up cargo they don't want anyone to know about."

"Let's go," Joe said.

"Right behind you."

I felt a tingle of excitement as we crept along the pier toward the shipyard. This could be it. The ship that had just pulled in could very well mean that the turtle-napper was waiting on the dock with Captain Hook, moments away from getting rid of the illicit cargo. I hoped the Chinese characters didn't confirm my fear that our turtle was destined for the medicine market.

We made it across the pier and took cover among stacks of old shipping containers, rusted metal tins the size of eighteen-wheeler truck trailers. The containers were stacked three and four high in some places, making the shipyard look like a tiny city made out of multicolor metal buildings. I wondered if one of them might be hiding Captain Hook.

I stepped forward to get a better look at the containers closer to the Chinese ship when Joe yelled out behind me.

"Look out!"

When I turned around, a metal crane hook the size of a Smart car was swinging straight at my face.

A METAL COFFIN 15

JOE

I TACKLED FRANK TO THE GROUND JUST AS the hook swung past his ear. It slammed into one of the containers with an earsplitting *BAM* that set the whole shipyard rattling.

Somebody was trying to kill us. That was actually a good sign. It meant we were on the right track.

We picked ourselves up off the ground and took off running as the hook swung back and slammed into the shipping container on the other side, barely missing us for a second time.

"I don't think this person likes us, bro!" I yelled as we ran.

"What gave you that impression?" he replied. I was too busy fleeing for my life to take the time to look, but I'm pretty sure he was rolling his eyes.

We leaped behind one of the containers as the hook swung past again. I peeked around the corner to see if I could glimpse who was driving the crane, but I didn't have a clear view. Whoever it was, they had us boxed in on three sides by shipping containers. We couldn't go back the way we came without exposing ourselves to the hook, but we were safe for the moment in our hiding spot. At least I thought we were.

"Uh-oh," Frank said.

I looked up. Uh-oh, indeed! The crane operator was trying a new strategy: using the hook to drop one of the huge cargo containers on top of us.

We were trapped with no option but to sprint back the way we came and try to outrun the falling forty-foot-long metal container. We both had the same reaction. . . .

"Runnnn!"

We did. The massive container began to give way with a shriek of grinding metal. Another second and it would be speeding down on top of us. There was no way we were going to make it.

"There!" Frank pointed.

He'd seen it an instant before I had. A partially open door in the shipping container to our right. We dove for it, tumbling over each other through the door as the shadow of the falling container swept over us. It crashed down to the ground and skidded into our new hiding place with the force of a tractor-trailer collision. We went flying, slamming off the metal walls like human pinballs. But when the dust settled (and there was a lot of dust), the Hardy boys were still alive.

"You okay?" I asked my brother.

"Relatively," he groaned.

"Then let's get out of here," I said.

The door had slammed shut in the collision. I lifted myself up and gave it a shove. And another. And another.

"Um, Frank, I think we have a problem."

The door wouldn't budge. Frank gave it a try. No dice.

"Okay, on three," he said.

"One . . . two . . . three!" We both shoved against the door with everything we had. But we might as well have been trying to push over the Empire State Building for all the good it did us.

I looked around the old container. Some light, and thankfully air, seeped in through small holes in its rusted side, but that was about all there was to see. It was sealed tight, with no way in or out except for the jammed-shut metal doors. It was also getting unbearably hot.

"If we're in here for too long, we'll either suffocate or bake to death," Frank said.

"Great," I said. "This case is determined to do me in one way or another."

Just then I heard the scraping of metal against metal outside the door, like someone was trying to pry it open. Frank and I exchanged a glance. Apparently our would-be killer wasn't content to wait for us to suffocate to death. He or she was going to break into the container and finish the job.

I scoped out the space for weapons to defend ourselves with. Nada. The only things inside the big metal box were two battered investigators and a whole lot of dust.

"If he has a gun, we're in trouble," I said. I always liked the Hardy boys' chances in a fight, but our wits and fists wouldn't do us much good if the bad guy had a weapon.

"Let's spread out," Frank said, and I nodded.

"No reason to give him an easy target."

Our attacker wouldn't know where we were, so he or she would have to take a second to assess the situation before launching an attack.

"And as soon as the door is opened . . . ," Frank began.

"We charge," I finished.

Frank and I braced ourselves, ready to rush the door like a couple of linebackers going for a quarterback sack. There was a clank followed by a clatter, and then the door swung open. A tall figure stood silhouetted in the doorway, holding what looked like a tire iron.

The first thing that registered was that he or she wasn't carrying a gun. The second was that the person appeared to be wearing a well-tailored suit. I knew it! Bishop!

I was about to charge when the figure stepped under the light. I was so surprised I stopped in my tracks. The man standing in the doorway of the container wasn't wearing a suit.

He was wearing a tuxedo.

It wasn't Bishop. It was Jonathan.

We'd been a little suspicious of Mr. V's butler, but I don't think either of us had really thought he was the criminal mastermind we were after. And, as we were about to find out, there was a good reason for that.

"If I had known I was going to have to rescue you, I would have worn a different tuxedo," Jonathan said.

Frank and I both relaxed, abandoning our planned charge. Jonathan wasn't there to hurt us. He was there to help us. Mr. V had been right about his butler's loyalty. Jonathan was one of the good guys.

"I overheard your conversation at the construction site and thought I might be able to provide some assistance," he said.

"It's a good thing you did, or we might have ended up rotting inside this thing like a couple of canned sardines," I said.

"But if you weren't the one operating the crane, who was?" Frank asked.

"And more importantly," I added, "where are they now?"

We were about to find that out too.

"Now if the young detectives will gather themselves, I think we have a turtle to find . . . ungh . . ."

Jonathan let out a moan and crumpled into a heap on the floor before he was able to finish. The tire iron clattered to the ground beside him in the doorway.

Someone standing in the shadows had just cracked Jonathan over the head with the butt of a flare gun.

I was so mad I couldn't even think straight. If Bishop had managed to get the best of us again, I was going to—

"I guess the old man knew what he was doing after all when he hired a couple of kids to find the thief," the villain said, stepping out of the shadows and into the light.

It turned out Carter had been right about the turtle-napper having a funny accent. Only it wasn't the one we were expecting.

"It's unfaahtunate yu'aah nevaah going to get the oppaah-tunity to shaah what yuh discovaahd."

That's how Ron Burris sounded when he said it in his thick New England accent—the one that Carter had mis-taken for British.

HUMAN CARGO

16

FRANK

WE'D BEEN SO QUICK TO LET OUR dislike for Dirk Bishop cloud our judgment that we'd automatically assumed that he was the accented kidnapper Carter had described. Two of the things our father, legendary detective Fenton Hardy, always tried to teach us about detecting are not to let your personal feelings about someone influence an investigation and never jump to conclusions without evidence. We'd done both, and now we were caught at the end of a flare gun because of it. I could only hope it wouldn't prove to be a fatal error.

If I'd taken more time to think about it, I might have realized that Carter could have mistaken the cadence of a thick New England accent for a proper English one. On the surface they may not sound the same, but there are definite similarities in the way Englanders and New Englanders drop some of their *R*s. It is called New England, after all. So it made sense that someone with an untrained ear might mix them up, especially if the voice was filtered through a distorter.

Not that any of that did us much good now that we were staring down the barrel of Ron Burris's flare gun.

Flare guns may not contain bullets, but fired at close range, one could be just as deadly. Not only did it shoot a large gunpowder-propelled projectile, it was designed to burst into flames. If it didn't kill us on impact, it would burn us to a crisp. Either way, we were basically toast if he decided to pull the trigger.

The best thing to do when you find yourself cornered by an armed assailant is to keep them talking to buy yourself time.

"You're not going to get away with this," I said, hoping I sounded more confident than I felt.

"Sure I am," he said. "Who's going to stop me? A couple of kids and an unconscious butler?"

He gave Jonathan's body a kick in the side. "I never liked you anyway, by the way."

"You want to come over here and try that on someone who can kick back?" Joe challenged.

Ron laughed. "Thanks for the offer, kid, but I'll pass. Why fight fair when you're the one holding the gun?"

I was disliking Ron Burris more and more by the minute.

"I have to say, though, I'm impressed," he said. "You made it a lot farther than I thought you would."

"Don't count us out yet," I told him.

"Tough talk, but I'm the one holding the gun, and . . ." Burris looked down at his watch. "Everything is right on schedule. In a few minutes, the turtle will be setting sail, and there's not a thing you can do about it."

"Where are you taking her?"

"To a land far away where rich people pay ridiculous sums of money for specimens as rare and interesting as our Captain Hook."

"You can't put her on a cargo ship! She may never survive the journey!" I said, but it only got worse.

"Unfortunately, you're right, but it's a risk I'm willing to take. My profit margin will take a big hit if she doesn't make it alive, but I can still make a nice score selling what's left of her to a traditional medicine trader, so it wouldn't be a total loss."

This was one of our worst fears: Captain Hook chopped up into parts.

"How can you even think about doing that? She's a living, breathing animal!" I shouted.

"She's also a very valuable commodity. Bradley might be happy throwing away millions and playing zookeeper, but I signed up for this job to make money, not lose it," Burris said, his tone growing harsher when he started talking about

Mr. V. "We're supposed to be running a business, not a charity, and not a personal piggy bank to fund the boss's childish hobbies. While the great Bradley Valledor is running around building his own private Sea World, our corporate profits are taking a beating. That means my bonuses are down along with the value of my stock options."

Burris gestured with the flare gun while he spoke.

"Which wouldn't be as bad if he treated me with some respect. I'm supposed to be a partner by now, not some underpaid, glorified gofer."

"Aw, poor you," Joc said. "It's still better than you deserve."

"Not so poor anymore," Ron shot back. "I've been looking for a chance to branch out on my own, and if Bradley isn't going to pay me what I'm worth, then I'll just have to get a little entrepreneurial."

"What you're doing isn't entrepreneurial, it's criminal," I said.

Burris shrugged. "You say turtle, I say turtle soup. With the money I get for this, I can kick my job to the curb and start my own PR firm. I saw an opportunity and I took it. It's just good business."

"It's good businessmen like you who are destroying our planet," I said.

"Not my problem, but hey, if it makes you feel better, I'll make a donation to the World Wildlife Fund in your name."

"You're a real class act," Joe muttered.

"I'm also about to be CEO of my own company," Burris retorted. "It's a trade-off I can live with."

"You're a disgrace to everything Mr. V believes in. I can't believe he would have been foolish enough to trust you with his plans," I said to Burris.

"Trust me? I'm surprised he hasn't fired me. He's rejected just about every piece of advice I've given him for months. Well, if he doesn't appreciate my talents, fine. I may not be a famous architect, but I've been in this business long enough to know my way around a blueprint. I had a hunch something funny was going on during the exhibit's construction, so I dug a bit deeper. You boys aren't the only ones around here who can play detective."

I really hated being compared to a scumbag like Burris. But if the guy was going to lay out his confession, I wasn't about to stop him.

"It's his own fault, really," Burris went on talking. "I've been warning Bradley about being more careful with his online security for years. But I'm just his PR director, what do I know about these things?" He chuckled. "It didn't take me long to hack into his computer, and there it was, his whole plan laid out for me like an all-you-can-eat endangered turtle buffet. I've got to give it to him, though. For a stubborn old fool, he really is a genius. Then again, so am I. I mean, he's the one at home sobbing into his giant fish tank, while I'm about to make a killing off his precious turtle."

I couldn't take it anymore. One more word out of Burris's smug grill and I was going to lose it. "Pretty proud of yourself, abducting a helpless animal, huh?"

"Yes, I am, thank you," Burris said. "In fact, I've already started ordering furniture for my new office to celebrate."

So that was the call Burris had taken outside the aquarium. He hadn't been discussing a client at all. This guy had been shameless, pretending to be concerned about Captain Hook one minute and buying office furniture with turtle blood money the next.

"Getting a little ahead of yourself, don't you think?" Joe said. "You know the saying about not counting your turtles before they hatch?"

"Clever." Burris smiled. "But you're right. That's why I'm not leaving anything else to chance."

He held up the flare gun to illustrate his point.

You remember what I said before about villains not confessing their plans to detectives unless they intend to permanently shut them up afterward? Well, this was the part where the bad guy tries to eliminate the witnesses—and I was pretty sure Ron wasn't going to just send us on our way. If we were going to get out of this, we were going to have to rely on ourselves.

"You'll only make things worse for yourself if you try to kill us, you know," I reasoned with him, hoping he had enough common sense not to add a murder rap to his list of crimes.

"Kill you?" He laughed. "What kind of person do you take me for? I'm not going to kill you. I'm going to lock you in this container and ship you to the other side of the world along with our turtle friend. I don't think the captain will mind some extra cargo."

"We'll suffocate if you leave us in here," I told him. "It's just as good as killing us yourself."

"Don't be silly," Ron said. "Captain Lau isn't going to let you die. Why would he do that when he can sell you as slave labor and make a nice profit?"

SHELL-SHOCKED

17

JOE

JUST WHEN YOU THINK THINGS CAN'T get any worse, the bad guy tries to sell you on the black market. I wasn't about to go quietly, but as long as Burris had that big old flare gun muzzle between us and the door, I didn't see how we were going to escape without being turned into fried fish.

Burris must have sensed we were thinking about trying something, because he decided not to waste any more time.

"Enjoy the trip, kids," he said. He dragged Jonathan's unconscious body outside the container and swung the big metal door shut.

CLANG. That was the sound of our fates being sealed.

Or was it? There was still a crack of light through the door where it should have been shut tight.

"What the—" I could hear Burris say through the other side of the door. He was trying to shove it closed, but it wouldn't budge the last couple of inches. That's because the tire iron Jonathan had been carrying was wedged in the corner. Jonathan had dropped it when Burris conked him on the head. Burris hadn't seen it. But we had.

"Now!" I yelled. Not that Frank needed the cue. He'd already launched into motion along with me the instant he realized the tire iron was stuck in the door. Burris saw us coming and jammed the flare gun through the opening in the door to shoot. Frank and I both slammed into the door at the same time, sending him flying backward before he had a chance to pull the trigger. We barreled through the door and out of the container into freedom. I never thought fishy air could smell so sweet.

Not that I had much time to savor it. Burris was back on his feet and diving for the flare gun he'd dropped in the container's doorway. I dove for it too. Burris got there first.

He grabbed the gun and stepped back as he lifted the weapon to shoot. He wasn't paying attention to where he had been standing, though, and tripped over Jonathan's body, tumbling backward through the door and into the container.

My brother and I leaped into action. I quickly reached my foot around and kicked the tire iron outside the container as

Frank slammed the door shut and threw the bolt, locking Burris inside.

Mr. V's butler had still managed to get revenge on Burris even though he was out cold. I'd have to make sure to thank him later when he woke up.

I think it took Burris a second to realize his predicament before he started banging on the door, demanding to be let out. Yeah, right. I had to smile.

"What do you think, bro? Should we see if Captain Lau has room on his ship for some additional cargo?" I asked Frank.

"Don't ships usually try to get rid of their human waste, not pick more up?"

"Come on, guys, you know I was just kidding about the slave labor thing, right?" I could hear Burris's muffled laugh from inside the container.

"Sure, Ron," I said back. "We were kidding too. We're turning you in to Chief Olaf, not Captain Lau."

"Be reasonable, guys. Can't we work out a deal? We'll split the proceeds from the turtle sale. You boys will be rich."

"Tell us where Captain Hook is, Burris," I said.

"Sure thing, guys, no problem, soon as you let me out. . . ."

"You're not going anywhere. Now where is she?" Frank demanded.

"Wait, wait, how about this? I give you guys the turtle and we can split the reward money. That's fair, right?"

I could tell he was pressed right up against the door,

so I gave it a good whack with the tire iron to set his ears ringing.

"Ow! Okay, okay, I take that as a no. You can keep the reward money. I don't need it. You can just let me out and I'll show you where the turtle is and we'll keep this whole misunderstanding between ourselves, okay? There's no need to even mention me."

"This isn't a negotiation. We just want the turtle," I said.

"As long as we each have something the other wants, it's still a negotiation," he said.

He had us there.

"You want to know where the turtle is and I want to get out of here, right?" he continued. "So I give you the turtle and you let me go free. You see, we're negotiating! Everybody wins!"

Even if we did take a chance and trust him to actually show us where Captain Hook was—which, by the way, we didn't—he still had that flare gun and was as likely as not to light us up like a couple of sparklers the second we opened the door.

"Come on, Joe," Frank said. "We're wasting our time."

"You're right, bro. He's not going anywhere. Let's go find—"

"Captain Hook, sirs," another New England accented voice said from behind us. It was Jonathan. "If you'll just follow me, she's this way."

Apparently our sneaky new butler friend had gotten up

without us noticing and done a little detecting of his own while we were dealing with Burris. We followed him to the dock, where there was a large wooden crate with airholes and the words FRAGILE—THIS END UP in big red letters.

Through the air holes we could see Captain Hook in the sad little tub Burris had stuck her in. She didn't look good at all.

I used the flattened end of the tire iron to pry open the crate. You could feel the heat and stench billow out as the panel tore away. Poor Captain Hook. It was like a stinky sauna in there. Burris hadn't even bothered to clean her water.

"She looks bad, Joe," Frank said. "Sea turtles overheat really easily. They can't control their own body temperature; they need the water to be just right in order to stay cool. We have to get her back to the aquarium fast or she could die."

Frank did a quick examination of Captain Hook to make sure she didn't have any open wounds. There weren't any cuts or scrapes to explain what we had assumed was her blood on the broken piece of coral Aly had found in the tank. But that would have to wait.

"I would offer to drive, but I'm not sure how we'd get her into the Rolls," Jonathan said.

"The quickest way is to bring her back the way she came," I said. "Through the tunnels."

Unfortunately, that also happened to be the most dangerous.

"You think you can find the way?" Frank asked.

"We're about to find out," I replied.

"What about them?" Jonathan asked, pointing to the cargo ship, which had pulled up anchor and wasn't wasting any time on its way back out to sea without its illicit reptilian cargo. Captain Lau must have gotten the hint that things weren't going according to plan when he saw a couple of teenagers and a butler liberating Captain Hook from her crate instead of Ron Burris.

"We'll let the coast guard deal with them. Right now we've got to get Captain Hook home," Frank said.

"Will you be okay?" I asked Jonathan. He had a nasty gash on the back of his head where Ron had conked him, and I'd be surprised if he didn't have a nice concussion to go with it.

"I have a hard head," Jonathan said. "Go on with Miss Hook. I'll keep an eye on Mr. Burris and make sure he's uncomfortable until we can summon the police."

We wheeled Captain Hook's tub back to the cannery and inside to the utility closet leading into the tunnel.

"If I'm right, this should take us back to the main tunnel running under the aquarium," I told Frank as I packed up the dive gear Burris had used to abduct Captain Hook from Predator Reef to take back with us.

"And if you're wrong?"

"Let's just hope I'm not."

Not that I wasn't a little nervous about it. And not that I was going to admit that to my brother. Luckily, I didn't have to. The tunnel under the cannery led back to the main tunnel like I suspected, and we were able to push Captain Hook, still in her tub, along the tracks back to the aquarium.

With Burris's dive gear and the gear I'd left in the tunnel, we were both able to suit up. Since I'd lost my regulator and my Octo had been damaged escaping from the shark, we were going to swim up together, with Frank using Burris's regulator and me breathing through the Octo attached to Burris's scuba tank.

As I helped Frank put on the tank, I noticed something—Burris's red scuba tank was all scuffed up and missing paint, almost as if it had scraped against a sharp object. Like, say, coral. I scraped my fingernail along the tank where it was scuffed. My finger came away smeared with a glob of dark red.

"What does that look like?" I asked Frank.

"Congealed blood," he answered. "I think we may have just solved another piece of the mystery."

"It would explain why Captain Hook doesn't have any open wounds," I said. "I'm betting the red stuff on the broken coral Aly found could be paint from a close call with Burris's tank and not blood at all."

Frank pointed to the holding tank above us. "You ready?"

"Let's do it."

It took some finagling, but we were able to use the hydraulic lift to scooch Captain Hook from the tub into the secret holding tank, climb in behind her, and shut the trapdoor under us. It was a tight fit, but all three of us made it.

When we pulled open the second trapdoor and the salt water from the exhibit flooded in, you could see Captain Hook revive almost instantly. It's like she knew she was home.

The three of us swam up together, with Captain Hook between Frank and me so we could help support her. She was still a little sluggish, but she gained more strength as she swam. I hadn't seen her swim before. It was amazing how well she moved with the hook-shaped shark-bitten flipper that had earned the turtle her nickname.

As we made our ascent to the tank's surface, reef fish swirled around like they were welcoming us home. Given our narrow escape from Ron Burris and nick-of-time rescue of Captain Hook, it was especially glorious.

As we rose, we saw something other than marine life too. Bright lights and tons of people were visible through the water's surface above us. Something was going on.

We surfaced in the center of the tank with Predator Reef's missing turtle only to find ourselves surrounded by a mob of people and cameras.

They couldn't have been expecting us, could they? No, they weren't even paying attention to what was in the water. Everyone was looking toward the front of the exhibit, where Chief Olaf was standing by a microphone, addressing the crowd. A few people spotted us and started murmuring excitedly, but not the chief. He just cleared his throat awkwardly into the mic and went right on talking.

"I'm sorry to report that we still haven't found the missing turtle," Chief Olaf sheepishly admitted to the crowd—totally oblivious to the fact that the missing turtle was just a few feet away with us!

I couldn't believe it. It looked like we had arrived right in the middle of a press conference announcing the police department's lack of progress on the case. A case we had just solved!

"I want to assure Bayport's citizens that we are working overtime and expect a break in the case soon—" Chief Olaf paused, distracted by the commotion that had been stirred up now that more people had seen us.

"What's going on there? Clear aside!" he ordered, gesturing for the reporters to get out of the way so he could see what everyone was looking at. When he saw us in the water with Captain Hook, he looked completely dumbstruck.

"Who . . . Frank and Joe Hardy?"

At first no one knew what to make of us popping up unannounced in the middle of the exhibit with Captain Hook, least of all Chief Olaf. Once the crowd realized we'd solved the mystery and put the turtle back in the turtle tank, the aquarium burst into cheers and the reporters started shouting questions.

"Way to go, boys!"

"Where was she?"

"Who took her?"

"How did you find her when the police couldn't?"

The chief didn't like that one.

"I thought I told you boys not to do anything without clearing it with me first," he bellowed.

"Sorry, Chief. Would you like us to take her back?" I asked as Frank and I treaded water with Captain Hook between us.

"No! I—of course not—but—you—I—" stuttered the chief. He looked like he didn't know whether to congratulate us or haul us in for questioning.

"Everyone clear aside," he said once he regained his composure. "Let's get the vets down here to check on the turtle."

When everyone turned their attention back to us, Chief Olaf sank into a nearby chair and let out a deep sigh. I'm not sure if he was happy that the case was solved or peeved because we'd been the ones to solve it instead of him . . . again.

There was another unhappy face waiting for us once we made it out of the tank. Dirk Bishop.

This time we kind of deserved the snooty look he gave us.

"It pains me to say this, but thank you," he said in his unmistakably British accent. "For finding the turtle, that is. I would have preferred it if the two of you had gotten lost in the process, but I am grateful nonetheless."

I winced. I guess we owed old Dirk an apology.

"Sorry, dude," I said. "We kinda had you mixed up with someone else."

"You most certainly did," Bishop said as he pulled an engraved crystal plaque from his briefcase. "You inquired before about the reason for my visit?"

He held up the plaque for us to inspect. The first thing we saw was the big Bayport Aquarium logo. Under that, it said, GOLD MEMBER AWARD—DIRK BISHOP—IN HONOR OF HIS GENEROUS CONTRIBUTIONS TOWARD THE ACQUISITION OF MARINE LIFE FOR PREDATOR REEF.

"Oops," Frank said.

"Oops, indeed," Bishop said, giving us the stink face as he walked off.

Oh well, I guess even brilliant detectives get it wrong sometimes.

There was someone else in the crowd who definitely was happy to see us, though.

"I'm sorry I was such a brat to you at my uncle's," Aly said, giving me an embarrassed smile. "I was pretty upset that he wouldn't let me help, and I guess I kinda took it out on you. I was really just worried about Captain Hook. Think you can forgive me?"

I gave Aly a big smile right back.

"It depends," I teased. "What are you doing tomorrow after I ace the big scuba exam?"

"Hmm, I don't know," she said. "But I wouldn't worry too much about the test. I think the instructor kind of likes you."

This time I knew that little sparkle in her eyes really was meant for me.

WHEN YOU'RE A KID,
THE MYSTERIES ARE JUST
THAT MUCH BIGGER . . .

NANCY DREW
AND
THE CLUE CREW
SECRET SAND SLEUTHS
All-new comics from
PAPERCUTZ™!